Brooke

BROOKE

V. C. Andrews ®

G.K. Hall & Co. • Chivers Press
Thorndike, Maine USA   Bath, England

This Large Print edition is published by G.K. Hall & Co., USA and by Chivers Press, England.

Published in 1998 in the U.S. by arrangement with Pocket Books, a division of Simon & Schuster Inc.

Published in 1999 in the U.K. by arrangement with Simon & Schuster Ltd.

U.S. Hardcover 0-7838-0329-X (Core Series Edition)
U.K. Hardcover 0-7540-1223-9 (Windsor Large Print)

The text of this Large Print edition is unabridged.
Other aspects of the book may vary from the original edition.

Set in 16 pt. Plantin by Rick Gundberg.

Printed in the United States on permanent paper.

British Library Cataloguing in Publication Data available

Library of Congress Cataloging in Publication Data

Andrews, V. C. (Virginia C.)
    Brooke / V.C. Andrews.
        p. cm.
    ISBN 0-7838-0329-X (lg. print : hc : alk. paper)
    1. Large type books. I. Title.
    [PS3551.N454B76 1998]
    813'.54—dc21   98-35890

Brooke

Prologue

When I first set eyes on Pamela Thompson, I thought she was a movie star. I was twelve, and I had shoulder-length hair the color of wheat. Most of the time, I kept it tied with the faded pink ribbon my mother had tied around it just before she dropped me off at the children's protection service and disappeared from my life. I wasn't quite two years old at the time, so I can't really remember her, but I often think of myself then as a top, spinning and spinning until I finally stopped and found myself lost in the child welfare system that had passed me from institution to institution until I wound up one morning staring wide-eyed at this tall, glamorous woman with dazzling blue eyes and hair woven out of gold.

Her husband, Peter, tall and as distinguished as a president, stood beside her with his arms folded under his camelhair overcoat and smiled down at me. It was the middle of

April, and we were in a suburban New York community, Monroe, but Peter was as tanned as someone in California or Florida. They were the most attractive couple I had ever met. Even the social worker, Mrs. Talbot, who didn't seem to think much of anyone, looked impressed.

What did two such glamorous-looking people want with me? I wondered.

"She has perfect posture, Peter. Look how she stands with her shoulders back," Pamela said.

"Perfect," he agreed, smiling and nodding as he gazed at me. His soft green eyes had a friendly twinkle in them. His hair was rust colored and was as shiny and healthy as his wife's.

Pamela squatted down beside me so her face was next to mine. "Look at us side by side, Peter."

"I see it," he said, laughing. "Amazing."

"We have the same shaped nose and mouth, don't we?"

"Identical," he agreed. I thought he must have poor eyesight. I didn't look at all like her.

"What about her eyes?"

"Well," he said, "they're blue, but yours are a little bit more aqua."

"That's what it always says in my write-ups," Pamela told Mrs. Talbot. "Aqua

8

eyes. Still," she said to Peter, "they're close."

"Close," he admitted.

She took my hand in hers and studied my fingers. "You can tell a great deal about someone's potential beauty by looking at her fingers. That's what Miss America told me last year, and I agree. These are beautiful fingers, Peter. The knuckles don't stick up. Brooke, you've been biting your nails, haven't you?" she asked me, and pursed her lips to indicate a no-no.

I looked at Mrs. Talbot. "I don't bite my nails," I said.

"Well, whoever cuts them doesn't do a very good job."

"She cuts her own nails, Mrs. Thompson. The girls don't have any sort of beauty care here," Mrs. Talbot said sternly.

Pamela smiled at her as though Mrs. Talbot didn't know what she was talking about, and then she sprang back to her full height. "We'll take her," she declared. "Won't we, Peter?"

"Absolutely," he said.

I felt as if I had been bought. I looked at Mrs. Talbot. She wore a very disapproving frown. "Someone will be out to interview you in a week or so, Mrs. Thompson," she said. "If you'll step back into my office and complete the paperwork . . ."

"A week or so! Peter?" she whined.

"Mrs. Talbot," Peter said, stepping up to her. "May I use your telephone, please?"

She stared at him.

"I think I can cut to the chase," he said, "and I know how eager you people are to find proper homes for these children. We're on the same side," he added with a smile, and I suddenly realized that he could be very slick when he wanted to be.

Mrs. Talbot stiffened. "We're not taking sides, Mr. Thompson. We're merely following procedures."

"Precisely," he said. "May I use your phone?"

"Very well," she said. "Go ahead."

"Thank you."

Mrs. Talbot stepped back, and Peter went into her inner office.

"I'm so excited about you," Pamela told me while Peter was in the office on the phone. "You take good care of your teeth, I see."

"I brush them twice a day," I said. I didn't think I was doing anything special.

"Some people just have naturally good teeth," she told Mrs. Talbot, whose teeth were somewhat crooked and gray. "I always had good teeth. Your teeth and your smile are your trademark," she recited. "Don't ever neglect them," she warned. "Don't ever neglect anything, your hair, your skin, your hands. How old do you think I am? Go on, take a guess."

Again, I looked to Mrs. Talbot for help, but she simply looked toward the window and tapped her fingers on the table in the conference room.

"Twenty-five," I said.

"There, you see? Twenty-five. I happen to be thirty-two years old. I wouldn't tell everyone that, of course, but I wanted to make a point."

She looked at Mrs. Talbot.

"And what point would that be, Mrs. Thompson?" Mrs. Talbot asked.

"What point? Why, simply that you don't have to grow old before your time if you take good care of yourself. Do you sing or dance or do anything creative, Brooke?" she asked me.

"No," I answered hesitantly. I wondered if I should make something up.

"She happens to be the best female athlete at the orphanage, and I dare say, she's tops at her school," Mrs. Talbot bragged.

"Athlete?" Pamela laughed. "This girl is not going to be some athlete hidden on the back pages of sports magazines. She's going to be on the cover of fashion magazines. Look at that face, those features, the perfection. If I had given birth to a daughter, Brooke, she would look exactly like you. Peter?" she said when he appeared. He smiled.

"There's someone on the phone waiting to speak with you, Mrs. Talbot," he said, and winked at Pamela.

She put her hand on my shoulder and pulled me closer to her. "Darling, Brooke," she cried, "you're coming home with us."

When you're brought up in an institutional world, full of bureaucracy, you can't help but be very impressed by people who have the power to snap their fingers and get what they want. It's exciting. It's as if you're suddenly whisked away on a magic carpet and the world that you thought was reserved only for the lucky chosen few will now be yours, too.

Who would blame me for rushing into their arms?

1

A Whole New Ball Game

In my most secret dreams, the sort you keep buried under your pillow and hope to find waiting in the darkness for you as soon as you close your eyes, I saw my real mother coming to the orphanage, and she was nothing like the Thompsons. I don't mean to say that my mother wasn't beautiful, too, wasn't just as beautiful as Pamela, because she was. And in my dream she never looked any older than Pamela, either.

The mother in my dreams really had my color hair and my eyes. She was, I suppose, what I thought I would look like when I grew up. She was beautiful inside and out and was especially good at making people smile. The moment sad people saw her, they forgot their unhappiness. With my mother beside me, I, too, would forget what it was like to be unhappy.

In my dream, she always picked me out from the other orphans immediately, and when I looked at her standing there in the doorway, I knew instantly who she was. She held her arms open, and I ran to them. She covered my face with kisses and mumbled a string of apologies. I didn't care about apologies. I was too happy.

"I'll just be a few minutes," she would tell me and go into the administrative offices to sign all the papers. Before I knew it, I would be walking out of the orphanage, holding her hand, getting into her car, and driving off with her to start my new life. We would have so much to say, so many things to catch up on, that both of us would babble incessantly right up to the moment she put me to bed with a kiss and a promise to be there for me always.

Of course, it was just a dream, and she never came. I never talked about her, nor did I ever ask anyone at the orphanage any questions about her. All I knew was she had left me because she was too young to take care of me, but in the deepest places in my heart, I couldn't help but harbor the hope that she had always planned to come back for me when she was old enough to take care of me. Surely, she woke many nights as I did and lay there wondering about me, wondering what I looked like, if I was lonely or afraid.

We orphans didn't go to very many places other than to school, but once in a while there was a school field trip to New York City to go to a museum, an exhibition, or a show. Whenever we entered the city, I pressed my face to the bus window and studied the people who hurried up and down the sidewalks, hoping to catch sight of a young woman who could be my mother. I knew I had as much chance of doing that as I had of winning the lottery, but it was a secret wish, and after all, wishes and dreams were really what nourished us orphans the most. Without them, we would truly be the lost and forgotten.

I can't say I ever even imagined a couple like Pamela and Peter Thompson would want to become my foster parents and then adopt me and make me part of their family forever. People as rich and as important as they were had other ways to get children than coming to an ordinary orphanage like this. Surely, they didn't go searching themselves. They had someone to do that sort of thing for them.

So I did feel as if I had won the lottery that day, the day I left the orphanage with them. I was wearing a pair of jeans, sneakers, and a New York Yankees T-shirt. I had traded a *Party of Five* poster for it. Pamela saw what the rest of my wardrobe was like and told Peter, "Just leave it. Leave everything from her past behind, Peter."

I didn't know what to say. I didn't have many important possessions. In fact, the only one that was important to me was a faded pink ribbon that I was supposedly wearing the day my mother left me. I managed to shove it into the pocket of my jeans.

"Our first stop," Pamela told me, "is going to be Bloomingdale's."

Peter brought his Rolls-Royce up to the front of the orphanage, and though I had heard of them, I had never actually seen one of them before. It looked gold-plated. I was too awestruck to ask if it was real gold. The interior smelled brand-new, and the leather felt so soft, I couldn't imagine what it must have cost. Some of the other kids were gazing out the windows, their faces pressed to the glass. They looked as if they were trapped in a fishbowl. I waved and then got in. When we drove away, it did feel as if I was being swept away on a magic carpet.

I didn't think Pamela literally meant we'd be going straight to Bloomingdale's, but that is exactly where Peter drove us. Everyone knew Pamela at the department store. As soon as we stepped onto the juniors floor, the salesgirls came rushing toward us like sharks. Pamela rattled off requests with a wave of her hand and paraded down the aisles pointing at this and that. We were there trying on clothes for hours.

As I tried on different outfits, blouses, skirts, jackets, even hats, Pamela and Peter sat like members of an audience at a fashion show. I had never tried on so many different articles of clothing, much less seen them. Pamela was just as concerned about how I wore the clothes as she was about how they fit. Soon I did feel as if I were modeling.

"Slowly, Brooke, walk slowly. Keep your head high and your shoulders back. Don't forget your good posture now, now that you're wearing clothes that can enhance your appearance. When you turn, just pause for a moment. That's it. You're wearing that skirt too high in the waist." She laughed. "You act like you hardly ever wear a skirt."

"I hardly do," I said. "I'm more comfortable in jeans."

"Jeans. That's ridiculous. There are no feminine lines in jeans. I didn't know the hems were that high this year, Millie," she said to the salesgirl helping me.

"Oh, yes, Mrs. Thompson. These are the latest fashions."

"The latest fashions? Hardly," Pamela said. "For the latest fashions, you would have to go to Paris. Whatever we have in our stores now is already months behind. Don't hold your arms like that, Brooke. You look too stiff. You look," she said, laughing, "like you're about to catch a baseball. Doesn't she, Peter?"

"Yes," he said, laughing along.

She actually got up to show me how to walk, to hold my arms, to turn and hold my head. Why was it so important to know all that when I was trying on clothes? I wondered. She anticipated the question.

"We really can't tell how good these garments will look on you unless you wear them correctly, Brooke. Posture and poise, the two sisters of style, will help you make anything you wear look special, understand?"

I nodded, and she smiled.

"You've been so good, I think you deserve something special. Doesn't she, Peter?"

"I was thinking the same thing, Pamela. What would you suggest?"

"She needs a good watch for that precious little wrist. I was thinking one of those new Cartier watches I spotted on the way into the store."

"You're absolutely right. As usual," Peter said with a laugh.

When I saw the price of what Pamela called a good watch, I couldn't speak. The salesman took it out and put it on my wrist. It felt hot. I was terrified of breaking or losing it. The diamonds glittered in the face.

"It just needs a little adjustment in the band to fit her," Pamela said, holding my hand higher so Peter could see the watch on my wrist.

He nodded. "Looks good on her," he said.

"It's so much money," I whispered. If Pamela heard me, she chose to pretend she hadn't.

"We'll take it," Peter said quickly.

What was Christmas going to be like? I wondered. I was actually dizzy from being swept along on a buying rampage that took no note of cost. How rich were my new parents?

I couldn't believe my eyes when I saw the house Pamela and Peter called home. It wasn't a house; it was a mansion, like Tara in *Gone with the Wind*, or maybe like the White House. It was taller and wider than the orphanage, with tall columns and what looked like marble front steps that led to a marble portico. There was a smaller upstairs porch as well.

The lawn that rolled out in front of the house was bigger than two baseball fields side by side, I thought. I saw fountains and benches. Two older men in white pants and white shirts pruned a flower bed that looked as wide and as long as an Olympic swimming pool. When we turned into the circular driveway, I saw that there was a swimming pool behind the house, and what looked like cabanas.

"How do you like it?" Pamela asked expectantly.

"Just you two live here?" I asked, and they both laughed.

"We have servants who live in a part of the house, but yes, until now, just Peter and I lived here."

"It's so big," I said.

"As you know, Peter is an attorney. He practices corporate law and happens to be active in state politics, too. That's why we were able to bring you home so soon," she explained. "And you already know that I was nearly Miss America," she added. "For many years, I was a runway model. That's why I know so much about style and appearance," she added without a tidbit of modesty.

"I think we've overwhelmed her, Pamela," Peter said.

"That's all right. We have so much to do. We don't have time to spoon-feed our lives to her, Peter. She's going to get right into the swing of things, aren't you, sweetheart?"

"I guess," I said, still gawking as we came to a stop.

Instantly, the front door opened, and a tall, thin man with two puffs of gray hair over his ears came hurrying out, followed by a short brunette in a blue maid's uniform with a lace white apron over the skirt.

"Hello, Sacket," Peter called when he stepped out of the car.

"Sir," Sacket replied. He looked to be in his fifties or early sixties. He had small, dark eyes and a long nose that looked as if it was still growing down toward his thin mouth and sharply cut jaw. The paleness in his face made the color in his lips look like lipstick.

"Welcome back, Mr. Thompson," he said in a voice much deeper than I had anticipated. It seemed to start in his stomach and echo through his mouth with the resonance of a church organ.

The maid flitted about the car like a moth, nervously waiting for Pamela to give her orders. She didn't look much older than thirty herself, but she was very plain, no makeup, her nose too small for her wide, thick mouth. Her nervous brown eyes blinked rapidly. She wiped her hands on her apron and stood back when Pamela stepped out of the car.

"Start bringing the packages in the trunk up to Brooke's room, Joline."

"Yes, ma'am," she said. She glanced at me quickly and moved around the vehicle to join Sacket at the rear. They began to load their arms with my packages.

"Peter, could you show Brooke the house while I freshen up?" Pamela asked him. She turned to me. "Traveling and shopping can make your skin so dry, especially when you go into those department stores with their centralized air. All that dust, too," she added.

"No problem, dear," Peter said. "Brooke," he said, holding out his arm. At first, I didn't understand. He brought it closer, and I put my arm through. "Shall we tour your new home?" he said, smiling.

I looked at the servants rushing up with my packages, the grounds people pruning and manicuring the flowers, hedges, and lawn, the vastness of the property, and my head began to spin. It all made me feel faint.

My new home?

All my life, I had lived in rooms no bigger than a closet, sometimes even sharing the space with another orphaned girl. I shared the bathroom with a half dozen other children most of the time. I ate in a cafeteria, fought to watch what I wanted to watch on our one television set, and protected my small space like a mother bear protecting her cubs.

Then, in almost the blink of an eye, I was brought to what looked like a palace. I couldn't speak. The lump in my throat was so hard, I felt as if I had swallowed an apple. I leaned on Peter's arm for real, and he led me up the stairs to the grand front door through which Pamela hurried as if the house were a sanctuary from the evil forces that would steal away her beauty.

"*Voilà,*" he said, standing back so I could step inside.

Once within the long entryway with tile floors that resembled chocolate and vanilla swirled ice cream, I turned in slow circles, gaping at the big oil paintings that looked as if they were taken from some European museum. I gazed at the large gold chandelier above us and the grand tapestry on the wall above the hallway, beside the semicircular stairway with steps covered in thick egg-shell-white carpet that looked as fluffy as rabbit fur.

"That's a scene from *Romeo and Juliet,*" Peter said, nodding at the tapestry. "The masked ball. You haven't read that yet, I suppose?"

I shook my head.

"But I bet you know the story, huh?"

"A little," I said.

"What do you think so far?" he asked.

"I don't know what to say. It's so big in here." I gasped, and he laughed.

"Close to ten thousand square feet," he bragged. "Come along."

At his side, I viewed the enormous living

room with its white grand piano.

"Neither of us plays, I'm afraid. Do you?"

I shook my head.

"Well, maybe we should think about getting you lessons. Would you like that?" he asked.

"I don't know," I replied. I really didn't know. I had never had a desire to play the piano. Of course, I would never have had an opportunity to learn, anyway.

"There are probably many new things you will find yourself wanting to do," Peter remarked thoughtfully. "When things seem so impossible, I imagine you don't give them a second thought, huh?"

I nodded. That made sense. He was smart. He had to be smart to have earned enough money for all of this, I thought.

There were many more expensive-looking paintings, very expensive-looking vases and crystal, and all of the furniture was spotless, the wooden arms and legs polished until they glittered, the sofas and chairs looking as if no one had ever sat on them.

"We don't spend enough time in here," Peter said as if he could read my thoughts. "It's one of those showpiece rooms. We're usually in the den, where we have our television set. Maybe now that you're here, we'll have some quality family time sitting and talking. It's a good room for talking, isn't it?" he asked with a smile.

"It makes me feel like I should whisper. It's like a room in a famous house or something," I said, and he laughed.

"I love to see the faces of those who view my home for the first time, because, through them, I can see it freshly myself," he said.

We continued down a hallway lined with mirrors in gilded, scrolled frames, small tables with vases full of fresh flowers, and paintings wherever there was free space.

"You have so many paintings," I said, as I stopped to study a beautiful seascape.

"Art's a good investment these days," Peter said. "You enjoy the beauty while it grows in value. That's better than some boring old corporate bond, huh?"

I shrugged. It was all a foreign language to me. He laughed.

"Pamela has about the same level of interest. She's one of those women who just want the machine to keep producing but don't care to know anything about the machine, which is all right," he added quickly. "I handle that part of our lives, and she . . . well, she's beautiful and makes me look good. Know what I mean?" he said with a wink.

Again, I had no idea, so I just smiled.

"Pamela is convinced you're going to be

just as beautiful as she is. You know, she really did almost make it to the Miss America pageant," he said.

"Really?"

"Uh-huh. First, she was prom queen, homecoming queen, Miss Aluminum Siding, something like that. Then, she was Miss Chesapeake Bay and a finalist for Miss Delaware, which would have taken her to the pageant. She lost out to the daughter of a very wealthy racehorse owner. The old fix was in there, I imagine," he said.

We stopped at the dining room. You had to have servants to eat a meal there, I thought. The oval dark cherry-wood table looked big enough to seat all the children in the orphanage, the administrators, cooks, custodians, and even some visitors. It had a dozen settings with goblets and wine glasses and more silverware than I saw in our whole cafeteria. There was a large matching hutch filled with glasses and dishes on one side and serving tables, highback chairs, a wall mirror, and two chandeliers as well.

"Dinner and all formal meals are served here, of course," Peter said with a sweep of his hand. "Pamela supervises everything in the house," he explained. "Her parents sent her to a finishing school, what some people call a charm school. She knows all there is to know about etiquette. You'll learn a lot from her. I swear," he said with a laugh, "she should have been born into royalty. She could live in that world. Our den or family room, as some refer to it," he continued, stopping at the next door on our right.

The furniture was black leather, and the television looked as big as some movie theater screens. Red velvet drapes were opened to reveal the pool and the cabana through large panel windows. A whole section of the room had its walls devoted to pictures of Pamela. I was drawn to them.

"There she is!" Peter cried. "Winning beauty contests, representing companies, riding in parades, meeting celebrities and important politicians, modeling designer clothes, which is how I met her."

I gaped. My new mother knew all these famous people?

Peter came to stand beside me. "Impressive, huh?"

"Yes," I said.

"I got lucky when she fell in love with me. She's a constant surprise. Pamela has her own kind of rare beauty, and she knows what beauty can do and cannot do," he said, nodding at me. "You're going to learn a lot of information that's practical for an attractive female," he promised. The way he spoke made it seem as if Pamela and now I, which I didn't believe for a moment, were citizens of a different country or part of a different species because of our looks. "She can be innocent and childlike when she has to and sharp, seductive, sophisticated, and keen when she has to, and she knows when to be which. Few women I know do, and that includes the brainy ones who work at my firm, the Ms. this and the Ms. thats," he said with some bitterness.

He seemed to become aware that he was getting too serious and smiled.

"That's a state-of-the-art digital sound system," he pointed out, "with Surround Sound. Few people have it, the technology is so new. Comfortable room, huh?"

I was listening with half an ear, part of me still awed at the luxuriousness in this overwhelming house. He continued the tour, showing me the two downstairs baths, servants' quarters, the kitchen, which looked big enough to handle a restaurant full of people, and the library, his office at home, which was dark and baronial with hundreds of leather-bound books.

"I'm afraid I'm unreasonable when it comes to my office. I don't permit anyone in here without me being present. Too many important documents and private papers," he explained. I saw a machine rolling out printed matter. "I get things faxed directly here sometimes. Well, now let's go upstairs and see your room."

I returned with him to the stairway and began to ascend. We heard what sounded like opera coming from a set of closed double doors at the end of the hallway.

"Pamela likes to listen to operettas while she's in her boudoir." When I made a face, he laughed. "You'll see."

We stopped at a tall door, and he glanced at me with that impish glitter in his eyes just before he opened it. This time, I couldn't swallow back my gasp.

The room, my room, was four times the size of what my room had been at the orphanage, and my bed was big enough to be a trampoline! It had four light pink posts and a headboard with a long-stemmed rose embossed on it. There was a milk-white desk with drawers and across the room a long counter with mirrors and a vanity table. The table was covered with brushes, containers of makeup, eyeliner, tubes of lipstick, a hair dryer, and an ivory box full of barrettes and hair ties.

All of my new clothes were put away in the dressers and large walk-in closet, and still there was room for lots and lots more. In the closet were mirrors and even a small table and chair.

On both sides of the bed were large windows draped in white and pink gingham curtains. My room looked out on a view of the countryside, and in the distance I could see a small lake.

Peter opened a cabinet across from the bed to show me a small television set. He then opened the bottom cabinet to reveal the sound system.

"We'll get you some music this weekend," he promised. "Pamela already has the next few days planned out, and shopping is a large part of it. So?" he said, standing there with his hands on his hips. "Are you happy?"

I shook my head. Happy just wasn't a big enough word. I turned around and then touched things to be sure they were all really there and this wasn't a dream.

"This is my room?" I finally had to ask.

He laughed. "Of course. Why don't you rest and then shower or bathe and dress for dinner, our first together. Pamela has had something special prepared. She's determined to spoil you rotten. She says a beautiful woman has to be spoiled. She must be right. After all, who can deny I have spoiled her?" he said.

There was a knock on the door, and we

turned to see Joline.

"Mrs. Thompson sent me to see if Miss Brooke would like me to run her bath now," she said.

Miss Brooke? I thought.

"See," Peter said, "how Pamela is always thinking ahead. Well?"

"Well what?" I asked.

"Would you like Joline to run your bath now?"

"Run my bath?"

"Get it ready for you?" Peter explained.

I gazed at the large, round tub in the sparkling bathroom. What was so hard about getting a bath ready?

"I can do that," I said.

"Of course you can," he said, "but from now on, someone else will do it for you. It's what Pamela wants. She wants you to be just like her."

Something nudged me deep down inside where all my dreams and secret thoughts were kept. It was like a tiny alarm. An alarm I didn't quite understand.

I gazed at my new clothes, my expensive watch, my whole new world, so much more privileged and safe than the orphanage.

What could possibly be the danger here?

2

Out with the Old

When Pamela had sent Joline to run my bath, she didn't mean simply to turn on the water. She instructed her on just how much of each of the bath powders and oils to mix as well. I stood by, watching her measure it all out with the precision of a chemist.

"What is all that?" I asked.

"These are things Mrs. Thompson says will keep your skin soft and silky and keep you from aging."

"Aging? I don't think I have to worry about aging. I'm not even thirteen," I said.

She smiled at me as if I had said something very stupid and then turned on the water. After that, she set out big fluffy bath towels and my robe and slippers.

"Is there anything else you need?" she asked me.

"No," I said. I couldn't imagine anything else to ask for.

"Have a nice bath," she said, and left.

Have a nice bath? I looked at the tub. At the orphanage, we usually took quick showers, and whenever we took a bath, that was in and out, too. Other people always needed to use the bathroom. What was I supposed to do in a bath except wash and get out?

I took off my clothes and folded my T-shirt over my jeans neatly, placing them on the counter by the sinks. Even though my clothes were old and worn, it seemed I should treat them special just because they were now here in a bathroom fit for a princess. I had two sinks! Why would one room have two sinks in its bathroom, and what was that bowl next to the toilet?

The rich marble tiles felt cool beneath my naked feet. I shut off the water. Bubbles had risen so high they threatened to spill over the edge of the tub. I stepped in and lowered myself gingerly. I don't know how she did it, but Joline got the water just right for me, not too hot, not too cold. It did feel good, and I had to laugh at myself reflected in the mirrors around the tub. There I was with only my head emerging from the small sea of bubbles.

Instead of a wash cloth, there was a sponge on a handle dangling from the shower rack. I ran it over my legs and sat back to rest my head against the soft, cushioned pillow attached to the bathtub. The soapy water snapped and crackled around me.

Could it be that fairy tales do come true? How much happier was Cinderella?

"There you are, a perfect fit," Pamela said as she came into my bathroom. She had her hair tied under a small towel and wore a long red silk bathrobe with Japanese letters drawn across the front. There was what looked like layers of thin mud over her cheeks and forehead. "How does it feel?"

"Very nice," I said, trying not to stare at her.

"Joline put in a little too much bubble bath, I see, but that's all right. We were born to indulge ourselves, you and I. Your indulgence was put on hold for a while, but that's over," she declared with the confidence of a queen. "Peter says you like your new home."

"It's a palace," I said.

She laughed. "Why not? We're a pair of princesses, aren't we? Don't you want to try the jets?"

"Jets?"

She bent down and pushed a brass button at the foot of the tub, and suddenly the water began to circulate madly, streams of it striking me in the legs and back. I screamed with delight, and she laughed. The bubbles grew bigger and bigger until I had to wipe them aside to see her standing there. She pressed the button again, and the jets stopped.

"I'll have to be sure to tell Joline she used too much bubble bath so she gets it right tomorrow night," she said.

"Tomorrow night?" Was I to take a bath like this every night?

"Of course. You have to cleanse the pores of your skin every day and rid them of the poisons. These gels and powders," she continued, pointing to the bottles and containers Joline had used, "are chosen with expert care. I have one of the best dermatologists in the country advising me on skin care. You're not going to get any of those ugly blemishes teenagers get," she vowed with such vengeance that my heart rose and fell. "Not my daughter, not the daughter of Pamela Thompson."

She pushed aside some of the bubbles and studied my hair.

"There's a lot of work to be done," she remarked as her fingers tested the strands. "Your hair feels like straw when it should feel like silk, and it needs to be thickened. I'll give you your first shampoo." She went to the counter to choose one. "We'll start with this," she decided. "Get your head wet."

I dipped myself down until my head went under water and then came up into her waiting hands. She poured the shampoo over me and began to scrub it in. I felt the ends of her long fingernails scratch at my scalp. A few times she hurt me, but I didn't complain. When she was done, she told me to dunk under the water again. I was surprised when her hands followed and continued to massage my scalp under the water, keeping me there until my lungs began to burn. I came up with a gasp.

She turned on a shower head attached to a short hose and rinsed me off. Then she returned to the counter to choose a conditioner. She worked that in and told me to let it set for a while.

"I've never really spent so long washing my hair before," I confessed. It seemed like a lot of work, anyway, and I couldn't imagine why it was important that your hair feel like silk instead of straw, but I didn't say that.

"You've got to do it every day from now on. You should try not to miss a day, even if you're sick. Beauty like ours can never be taken for granted, Brooke. Did you ever hear of antitoxins?"

I shook my head.

"Toxins age you, but there are antitoxins to battle them and keep us from getting old too fast. I intend never to look my age, even if I have to fight it with plastic surgery. I know what you're thinking," she said before I uttered a sound. "You're thinking I already have had plastic surgery, right?"

I shook my head.

"How else could I look like a teenager or a woman just twenty, right?"

"I don't even know what plastic surgery does," I confessed.

She wasn't listening. "Plastic surgery is the artificial last resort," she lectured. "It's for the lazy. If you watch your diet, exercise, and nurture your skin the way you and I do, there is no reason to go under the knife."

"Should I get out now?" I asked. I didn't want to interrupt her, but the water was getting cold.

"What?"

"Should I get out of the bathtub?"

"Oh, first we want to rinse out your conditioner," she said, and went to the small hose again. "From now on, you'll be able to do this yourself, and if you're too tired, you can have Joline do it."

"This is the first time anyone's washed my hair that I can remember," I said. "I imagine they did when I was a baby."

"You're always a baby when it comes to being pampered, especially by men. Never, never let them believe they've made you happy," she advised.

"Why not?"

"They'll think they've done enough. They

can never do enough. That's our motto. Okay, step out," she said, and I rose.

"Just as I thought. You have a perky little figure, not an ounce of baby fat," she remarked. "Actually," she said, letting me stand there naked and not handing me my towel, "you're a bit more muscular than I expected. We don't want to be too hard," she warned as she pinched the muscle in my thigh. "Men like their women to feel like women," she said.

She handed me the towel finally, and I wrapped it around myself quickly, drying my body as she studied me. She looked at my pile of clothes.

"Weren't you wearing a bra?" she asked.

"No."

"Your breasts are forming. It's never too early for a woman to worry about sagging," she declared. "First thing we do tomorrow is buy you more underthings. Sit at the table, and I'll dry and brush out your hair."

"Thank you," I said, and sat with the towel still wrapped around me.

She started the blow dryer and ran the brush through my hair. "It's nice having someone else to nurture and develop. It's as if I'm starting over. Of course, I couldn't do this with just anyone. I had to have a young girl who had promise. I'm just surprised at the size of your shoulders," she muttered. "I wonder why I never noticed they were so broad."

"My shoulders?"

"How did you get them to be so . . . manly? You don't do those exercises with weights, do you?"

I shook my head. What was wrong with strong shoulders?

"I suppose it's just something that happened. I'm sure it will change as your hormones do. And we can help them along," she whispered in my ear.

"We can what?"

"Make our female hormones more efficient. I have some pills, some nutritional supplements my nutritionalist has provided. I'll tell you all about it. Oh, there's so much to do. Isn't this fun?" she said. "See how much nicer your hair feels? Go on, touch it," she said, and I did. It did feel softer. I nodded.

"You're going to be a contestant faster than you think," she said.

"A contestant?"

"For the beauty pageants." She laughed. "Maybe I'll enter you in Miss Teenage New York this year. Yes, I will," she decided instantly. "And you'll win, too. Think of what they will say." She stepped back. The headlines flashed across her eyes as she envisioned them and drew them in the air with the brush. " 'Pamela Thompson's daughter declared Miss Teenage New York.' I love it."

I stared at her reflection in the mirror. She was still fantasizing some scene on a beauty pageant stage. My eyes went to the toilet again. "What's that?" I asked.

"What?" She looked. "Oh, that's a bidet. Don't you know what that is?" I shook my head. "You poor thing. That's to keep us clean in our private place," she said. "You have to do it every day, too. Women don't realize how they can . . . smell."

I looked at it, my eyes wide.

"It feels good, too," she said. She laughed. "Men want that to be the healthiest place on our bodies, but I bet you know all about that, don't you?" she asked guardedly.

"No," I said, "not really."

"Not really?" She stared at me a moment. "You're a virgin?"

"Uh-huh," I said, amazed that she would even ask.

"What a wonderful idea," she declared, "to be virginal until you win your first big pageant. I love it. You must promise me you'll not give yourself to just any old boy, Brooke. Sex is your treasure," she advised. "You must guard it like a dragon who guards the pots of gold in its cave, okay? We'll talk a lot more

40

about this. That's what mothers are for. I'm a mother," she declared, gazing at herself in the mirror. "Who in his right mind would look at me and think, even for a moment, that I was old enough?" She laughed, and then her gaze went to my clothes again.

"We've got to get rid of those. I'm sorry you brought them in here," she said.

"What?" I asked.

She picked up my T-shirt and jeans as if they were diseased.

"Ugh. They still reek of that horrible place. I hate jeans on a girl, anyway."

She opened a drawer and took out a pair of scissors. Before I could utter a protest, she jabbed the scissors into the seat of my jeans and tore a gash through them. Then she pulled them apart and threw them and my T-shirt on the floor.

"Just leave it there for Joline to put in the garbage," she said.

She washed her hands as if she had been handling contaminated clothing and then smiled at my shocked face.

"Time to pick out something to wear to dinner," she said. "We want to look beautiful together when we enter and Peter looks up from the table. We want to take his breath away. From now on, every time we walk into a room together, we want to captivate our

41

audience. That," she declared with a sharp nod, "is what we were placed on earth to do."

Before I followed her out to the bedroom, I went to my jeans and took out my hair ribbon, thankful to see that it hadn't been cut in two. I clutched it tightly in my hand, and as she sifted through all my new clothes, I shoved it into a dresser drawer. I was afraid she might want to throw that out, too.

"No, no, no, maybe, yes," she declared, and plucked the blue dress off its hanger. "Try this," she said, handing it to me, and stood back.

Why did she have to see it on me again? I wondered. She had seen it on me in the store. She knew what it looked like.

"Don't you think you should put on a pair of panties first?" she asked with a smile when I dropped the towel and reached for the dress.

I nodded and went to the dresser drawer. After I put the panties on, I slipped the dress over my head and pulled it down. It fit a little snugly and had wide straps and a U-shaped collar. I turned to face her, and she grimaced.

"I don't know why I didn't notice it before, but your shoulders and arms are so . . ."

"What?" I asked.

"Manly," she repeated. "I'll have to speak to my doctor about you. There must be a way to get you to look softer," she decided. "Now you see why clothes are like living things."

I shook my head.

"They take on different personalities in different environments. Back at the department store, under those harsh lights, colors were washed out, and the garments appeared one way, but here, in a warmer setting, in a bedroom or in a dining room, they're different. I wouldn't have bought this one," she concluded. "From now on, I'm going to have them bring your clothing here to try on."

"Bring them here? You mean to my room?"

"Of course," she said. "We were all just in too big a rush. But" — she recovered with a smile — "no harm done. We'll buy some more. That's all. I have a blue dress to wear, too. How experienced are you with makeup?" she asked.

"I put on lipstick sometimes," I said.

"Lipstick?" She laughed. "Sit at your table. Go on. Quickly. I have my own hair to style and my own makeup to do yet."

Why were we getting so dressed up for dinner? I wondered. Were there more people coming? Was it going to be like a party?

I sat, and she came up behind me. She turned on the magnifying mirror, and the light washed away any shadows on my face. Then she pressed her palms against my cheeks and turned my head from side to side, studying me.

She nodded. "Now that I have you under the light, I see where we have to make your nose look smaller. I want to highlight your eyes and thicken your lip line just a little."

She began to work on me as if I were being made up for a ball. The surprise in my face was easy to see. I was never very good at disguising my feelings. Whenever I thought something was stupid, the corners of my mouth turned up in a smirk that gave my feelings away. One of my grade-school teachers, Mrs. Carden, once told me that my forehead was as good as a blackboard on which my thoughts appeared in bright, white, chalky letters.

"Every time you go out of this room, and especially every time you leave this house," Pamela lectured, "you have to remember you are onstage. A woman, a real woman, is always performing, Brooke. Every man who looks at you is your audience. Whether we like it or not, we're attractive, and that means men's eyes are like little spotlights always turned on our faces and bodies.

"And even if you're married for ages or going with some beau for months, you still have to surprise him with your elegance and beauty every time he sets eyes on you, understand?"

"Why?" I asked.

"Why?" She stopped working and put her hands on her hips. "Why? Because if we didn't, they would look elsewhere, for one, and because we want to be the center of their attention always. Wait, just wait," she continued, returning to the makeup, "until you're out there, competing. You'll see. It's a cutthroat, ruthless world when it comes to winning the affections of men. Every woman, whether she wants to admit it or not, is competing with every other woman. When I walk into a room, who do you think looks at me first? The men? No. Their wives look at me and tremble.

"I have the feeling," she concluded, "that I found you just in time. You're still young enough to develop good habits. Press your lips together. There," she said. "Let's look at you now."

She turned my head toward the mirror and stood behind me again, her hands moving me so that she could get a profile.

"See the difference? You walked in here a child, and now you look like a young woman, which is what I'm going to make you into."

I stared at myself. With the eyeliner, the rouge, the lipstick, I did look entirely different, but I wasn't sure I liked it. I felt clownish. I was afraid to utter a word, and I was terrified that my blackboard of a forehead would write out my disapproval. If it did, she didn't notice, maybe because she had covered it in makeup.

"Don't think you have to spend a lot of time in the sun to get your skin this shade, Brooke. The sunlight is devastating. Those horrible ultraviolet rays age us. We don't need it with this makeup, anyway. Well now, you look ready. Come along and talk to me while I get dressed."

I rose and started after her.

"Wait," she said with a harshness I hadn't heard before. "You weren't planning on walking around *barefoot*, were you?" The way she said *barefoot* made it sound like a sin.

"What? Oh," I said, looking down.

"Put on the shoes that match the dress," she ordered sternly.

I went to the closet and stared at the dozens of pairs she had bought me.

"The pair second from the right," she said impatiently. "You have so much to learn. Thank goodness I came along."

I put on my shoes and followed her out, glancing through my bathroom doors at my torn jeans and my T-shirt lying on the floor where she had thrown them. It was like saying good-bye to an old friend. Dressed in my expensive clothes, my hair styled, my face made up, I felt as if I had betrayed someone. Myself?

"Come on," she urged when I hesitated. "Peter is already downstairs. Of course, we must always keep men waiting. That's a golden rule. Never be on time, and never, never, never be early. The longer they are made to wait, the more their anticipation builds, and the louder the applause in their eyes," she said. "Now, get moving. I need time to make myself more beautiful, too."

I hurried after her, and when she opened the double doors to the master bedroom, I felt the breath spiral up from my lungs and get caught in my throat like a giant soap bubble. It wasn't a bedroom; it was a separate house!

There was a long carpeted landing that led to two steps. On the right was a living room with furniture and a television set. On the left was a bedroom that surely was fit for a queen. It was round and had its own white marble fireplace, but what was astounding to me was the bed, because it, too, was round with big, fluffy pillows. Above it was a ceiling of mirrors. There were mirrors everywhere. I gaped.

Pamela saw my amazement and laughed.

"Maybe now you'll understand what I meant when I said we were always on the stage, always performing, Brooke." She looked at the bed and then up at the ceiling. "You know what it's like?" she asked, her voice softer but full of passion.

I shook my head.

"It's like we're in our own movie, and you know what?"

I waited, afraid to breathe.

"We're always the stars," she said, and laughed.

3

All the World's a Stage

Pamela had me sit beside her at her vanity table. It was designed so that the mirrors weren't only in front of her. They followed the curve of the wall and surrounded her. She could glance to the right or left and see her profile without moving her head. She said it was important that she know how she appeared from every angle, every side, and especially the rear. "When they see how fabulous I look from behind," she explained, "they'll be dying to see my face."

She spoke to me in the mirror instead of turning to look at me directly. It was as if we were looking at each other through windows.

"Always call me Pamela," she told me. "It's nice to have a daughter, and I want to be known as your mother, but I'd rather people thought we looked more like sisters, wouldn't you?" she asked.

I nodded even though I wasn't sure. I had

friends at the orphanage, girls who were so much like me we could have been sisters. We shared clothes, did schoolwork together, sometimes talked about boys and other girls at school who often snubbed us because we were from the orphanage. Together we battled, and together we suffered. For the first time, I thought of the life I'd left behind and how I would miss it.

But what I never had was someone older, someone motherly to whom I felt I could turn, not with complaints but with questions, more intimate questions, questions I didn't feel comfortable asking my counselors or teachers. Not being able to have someone like that left me feeling even more alone, listening to the echo of my own thoughts.

"These women who have children early get to look so matronly even when they're barely out of their twenties. It's all about attitude, and attitude is very important, Brooke. It will have a direct effect on your appearance. If you think of yourself as older, you'll look older. I think of myself as becoming even more beautiful, just blossoming," she said, smiling at her image in the mirror. She looked at me.

"I don't want you to think I didn't want children. I just couldn't have them while I was in competition and while I was a model. Having children changes your shape. Now," she said, smiling, "I still have my shape, *and* I have a daughter."

She wiped the thin layer of brown facial mud off gingerly with a dampened sponge and then stared harder for a moment and leaned in toward the glass. Her right forefinger shot up to the crest of her left cheek as if she had just been bitten by a bug. She touched it and then turned to me.

"Do you see a small redness here?" she said, pointing to the spot.

I looked. "No," I said.

She returned to the mirror, studied herself again, and then nodded.

"It's not something an untrained eye would see," she said, "but there's a dry spot here. Every time I go out of this house, I come home with something bad."

She looked over the rows of jars filled with skin creams and lotions. Her eyes turned a bit frantic when she lifted one and realized it was empty.

"Damn that girl. I told her to keep this table stocked, to check every day and replace anything that was empty or even near empty," she said, rising. She went to the closet on her right and opened the door.

When she stepped to the side, I saw the shelves and shelves filled with cosmetic supplies. It looked as if she had her own drugstore. She plucked a jar off a shelf and returned to her table.

"This has special herbal ingredients," she began. "It replenishes the body's natural oils." She dipped her fingers into the jar and smeared the gooey-looking, chalky fluid over her cheek, gently rubbing it into her skin. Then she wiped off the residue and looked at herself again.

"There," she said, turning to me. "See the difference?"

I saw no changes, but I nodded anyway.

"Your skin is very sensitive to atmospheric changes, my dermatologist says. It was so hot in that orphanage, for example, and then we went to that air-conditioned department store, but they don't filter their air conditioners enough, and there are particles floating around that stick to your skin and begin to break down the texture.

"The water in this house is specially filtered," she continued. "Harsh minerals are removed so you don't have to worry about baths and showers."

It had never occurred to me ever to worry about such a thing, anyway.

"Our air conditioners, heaters, everything is filtered. Other people's homes are filled with dust. Sometimes I feel like wearing a surgical mask when we're invited to someone's house, even Peter's wealthiest clients. They just don't know, or they just don't care about the beauty regimen," she railed.

She sighed as she began to brush out her hair.

"These ends are splitting again. I told my stylist he wasn't trimming it right. Damn," she said, and then stopped. "See that, see?" she said, pointing at her face. "Whenever I get upset, that persistent wrinkle shows itself just under my right eye. There, see?"

There was a very tiny crease in her skin, but I would never call it a wrinkle.

She took a deep breath, closed her eyes, and sat there quietly for a moment. I waited until she opened her eyes again.

"Anxiety, aggravation, worry, and stress hasten the aging process. My meditation instructor has taught me how to prevent it. I must chant and tell myself I will not be upset. But it's so hard sometimes," she moaned.

She stared at me.

"You shouldn't squint like that, Brooke. See how your forehead wrinkles? It's never too early to think about it. Do you need glasses?"

"I don't think so," I said.

"Don't worry about it if you do. We'll get you the best contact lenses. Peter wears contact lenses."

"He does?"

"He's a good-looking man, your new father, isn't he?" she asked with a proud smile. "I didn't just marry for money and position. I married a handsome man."

"Yes, he is handsome," I agreed.

"And he's a good lover, too, a considerate lover. He won't even think of kissing me until he's shaven. A man's beard can play havoc with your complexion. If a man is selfish, if all he cares about is his own sexual gratification, you'll feel used. I'm nobody's possession. I'm nobody's toy," she declared hotly as if someone had just accused her of being so. Whenever anger flashed across her face, her nostrils widened and her eyes looked as if tiny candle flames were burning behind them.

She paused and looked at me hard again. "How much do you know about sex? I know you're a virgin. You told me so, and I believe you. I hope we'll never lie to each other," she added firmly. "How close have you come? Did you have one steady boyfriend?" She fired her questions in shotgun fashion.

"I've never had a boyfriend," I said.

Disbelief filled her face. "From what I saw, the living quarters were quite close. Boys and girls shared so much, and there wasn't all that much supervision, was there? I mean, there must have been plenty of opportunities for hanky-panky. You can be honest with me,

Brooke. I'm your mother now, or your mentor, I mean," she quickly corrected.

"I never had a boyfriend. Really," I said.

"But you know things, don't you?" she asked, nodding. "You know what they want, what they always want, no matter how they present themselves or what they promise. Men see you as one thing and one thing only, whether you're a prom queen or a member of the Supreme Court, Brooke, and you know what that is?"

I shook my head.

"A vessel of pleasure into which they can dip."

She returned to her makeup. "Satisfying their little telescopes," she muttered.

"Their what?"

She laughed. "Telescopes." She looked at me. "Don't tell me you've never seen one of those."

"I've seen them," I said, recalling different occasions when I had caught sight of one of the boys in the bathroom.

"So you know they come out like a telescope when they are aroused. At least, that's how I always think of them," she said, laughing. "Oh" — she squealed with delight — "isn't it going to be fun for me to experience everything again through you? That," she said, growing serious, "is why it's so important you do everything I tell you and benefit from my knowledge, especially when it comes to men. What else is more important, anyway?" She shrugged. She gazed at her large, rich surroundings. "After all, my knowledge got all this.

"And," she added, turning back to me, this time with her eyes so intense she scared me, "with my help, you will get everything, too."

Peter was sitting quietly in the dining room, waiting for us. The moment we came through the door, he rose, his face lighting up with happiness.

"You can do wonders, Pamela," he declared. "Look at her. She really is a younger version of you."

Pamela's look of satisfaction grew icy instantly. "Not so much younger, Peter," she admonished.

"No, no, of course not. It's just that she came into the house a little girl, and you've turned her into a young lady in a matter of hours," he quickly explained. He hurried to pull the chair out for her, and she sat. Then he did the same for me. I sat across from Pamela on Peter's left, and she sat on his right. There was still so much table left, I felt silly.

"I have a lot to teach her," Pamela explained.

"I told her so, and I told her there was no better woman for the job, didn't I?" he asked me. I nodded.

Pamela seemed placated. She relaxed and smiled. Seemingly out of the walls, music flowed, soft, pleasant sounds. Sacket came in with a bottle of champagne in a bucket of ice and set it down beside Peter.

"Have you ever had champagne before, Brooke?" Peter asked me.

"No," I said. "I had a sip of beer once."

He laughed.

Pamela made a small smile with her lips. She looked as if she could orchestrate every tiny movement in her face, every feature to move independently of the others.

Peter nodded at Sacket, and he poured just as much in my glass as he did in Peter's and Pamela's. Then he placed it back in the bucket and left. Peter raised his glass slowly.

"Shall we make a toast, Pamela?"

"Yes," she said.

"To our new daughter, our new family, and the beautiful women in my life," he added.

We all touched our glasses. I had seen this only in the movies, so I was very excited. I sipped my champagne a little too fast and started to cough.

"You took in too much," Pamela said. "Just let your lips touch the liquid, and permit only

57

the tiniest amounts into your mouth. Everything you do from now on must be feminine, and to be feminine you need to be dainty, graceful."

I crunched the napkin in my hand and wiped my mouth.

"No, no, no," she cried. "You dab your mouth, Brooke. This isn't a hot dog stand, and even if it was, you wouldn't do that. It looks too manly, gross." She shook her head to rid herself of the feeling. "Go on," she insisted. "I want to see you do it right. That's it," she said when I dabbed my lips so gently I hardly touched the napkin. "Perfect. See?" She looked at Peter.

"Yes," he said. "She's going to do just fine. How do you like your champagne?" he asked me.

I shrugged. "I thought it would be sweeter."

"It's not a Coke," Pamela said. "Besides, sugar is terrible for your complexion. You'll see that we have no candy in our house and that our desserts are all gourmet when we have them. We're both very conscious of calories normally, but tonight, being it's so special, we're indulging ourselves," Pamela explained.

Joline came in with our salad. I watched Pamela to see which fork to use because there were three. Peter saw how I was studying their every move and smiled.

"Every moment of your life in this house will be a learning experience," he promised. "Just follow Pamela's instructions, and you'll do fine."

Our salad was followed by a lobster dinner. Sacket brought out wine, and I was permitted some of that as well. Everything was delicious. The dessert was something called crème brûlée. I hadn't even heard of it, much less ever tasted it, but it was wonderful. Everything was.

Afterward, we went into the family room to talk, but Pamela seemed very fidgety. She excused herself and went upstairs. I wondered what was wrong, and when Peter was called to the phone, I decided to look in on her. I hurried up the stairs and knocked on her door. She didn't answer, but I heard what sounded like someone vomiting. I opened the door and looked in.

"Pamela?" I called. "Are you all right?"

The sounds of regurgitating grew louder and then stopped abruptly. I heard water running, and a moment later, she stepped out of the bathroom. Her face was crimson.

"Are you all right?"

"What's wrong?" she asked.

"I thought I heard you being sick."

"I'm fine," she said. "Did Peter send you up?"

"No."

"I'm fine," she insisted. "Just go back downstairs and continue to enjoy your evening. I'll be right there. Go on," she ordered.

I left, closing the door quietly behind me.

If she was sick, why was she so ashamed? I wondered.

Minutes later, she rejoined Peter and me, and she looked as perfect as she had when she had come downstairs for dinner. She was certainly not sick, I thought, not the way I knew sick people to be. Peter didn't notice anything wrong, either.

He asked me lots of questions about my life at the orphanage. Pamela was more interested in what I remembered about my mother.

"Nothing, really," I said. "All I have is a faded pink ribbon that I was told was in my hair when she left me."

"You still have it? Where? I didn't see it when you came here," Pamela said quickly. She looked at Peter fearfully.

"It was in the pocket of my jeans," I said. "I put it in my dresser drawer."

"Why would you want to keep something like that?"

"I don't know," I said, near tears.

"It's nothing, Pamela. A memory," Peter

said, shrugging. She looked unhappy about it and settled back in her chair slowly.

"There are all these horror stories about families who have taken in a child, and years later, the biological mother, a woman who had nothing to do with raising the child, comes around and demands her rights," Pamela muttered.

"That can't happen here," Peter assured her. "She doesn't even remember her face. Do you, Brooke?"

I shook my head. "No."

"You shouldn't hold onto anything, not even a ribbon," Pamela said angrily. "The woman got rid of you like . . . like some unwanted puppy."

"You're upsetting her, Pamela," Peter said gently.

She looked at me and relaxed again. "I'm just concerned about you. I want you to be happy with us," she explained.

I tried to smile. This whole day was so overwhelming, so full of surprises and excitement, I couldn't keep my eyes open. Peter laughed and suggested I get a good night's rest.

"It's all just starting for you now, Brooke. This has only been a taste of what's to come," he promised.

"I'll come up with you and show you the proper way to take off your makeup," Pamela said, "and then give you something to put on your face."

"Put on? But I'm going to sleep," I said, confused.

"That's when your body is best able to replenish itself," she explained. "You want to wake up looking beautiful, don't you?"

Peter laughed. "Just listen to Pamela," he said. "You can see she knows what she's talking about."

Put on makeup every day, wash with special soaps, filter your air, eat a special diet, avoid being upset, chant, meditate, put something special on while you slept. It seemed like so much effort. If this is what I had to do to be beautiful, I thought, I think I'd rather be plain old me.

But I would never say so, not if I wanted Pamela to love me like a daughter or even a sister.

I knew that much, but what I didn't know was that what I knew was not enough, not hardly enough.

4

Secrets

For the next few days, Pamela took over my life as if I had nothing more to say about it. She set schedules for almost every waking moment and left nothing to chance. The plan was to enroll me in the Agnes Fodor School for Girls, a private school designed only for those born with silver spoons in their mouths. However, before I could be brought to the school for registration, Pamela wanted me to learn enough about poise, etiquette, and style to "fool any of the blue bloods."

"Blue bloods," she explained, "are those who are born into wealth and position, whose family lineage goes back to the most respectable and important people in our social and political history. They are taught from day one how to behave and conduct themselves, and that is how I want you to appear, as well."

"But I'm not a blue blood," I pointed out.

"You are now," she said. "Peter and I come

from the best stock, and you will carry our name. Most important, when someone looks at you, they'll be looking at me. Understand?"

I nodded, but I didn't like it. I didn't like becoming an instant blue blood. I needed more time to get used to having servants at my beck and call and more time to learn my way about a house that resembled a palace. I didn't like Joline drawing my bath every night and laying out my nightgown and slippers. I felt like an invalid. Pamela decided what colors I would wear and how I should brush my hair. When I said I had never worn nail polish, she looked at me as if I was some sort of alien creature.

"Never? I just can't believe that," she said.

When I laughed at the idea of polishing my toenails, she grew angry. "It's not funny. It's as serious as any other part of your body," she insisted.

"But who will see them?" I asked.

"It's not important who else sees them. You must understand. We're beautiful first for ourselves, to make ourselves feel special, and then, when we feel special, others will see it and think of us as special, too."

"I don't understand why we would be so special," I muttered.

"Your clothes, your coiffure, your makeup, your walk, and your smile, everything about you must coordinate, must work together. Women like us," she taught me, "are truly works of art, Brooke. That's what makes us special. Now do you understand?" she asked.

I didn't, but I saw that if I didn't look as if I did, she would grow angry.

The one time she did get very angry with me occurred three days after I had arrived, when I asked if I could call someone at the orphanage. I wanted to talk to Brenda Francis, my one close friend. I knew she missed me. I was practically the only one she spoke to, and I wanted to see how she was doing. I had left so quickly, we never really had time to say good-bye.

"Absolutely not!" Pamela said forbiddingly. "You must drive that place and everyone in it out of your memory forever.

"Very soon," she continued, "you will completely forget that you were ever an orphan." She clenched her teeth and grimaced as if pronouncing the word *orphan* filled her mouth with castor oil.

Deep inside my heart, I worried that if my new mother found orphans so distasteful, how could she ever come to love me? Maybe she was worried about that, too, and that was why she was so intent on my becoming a new person as soon as possible. For both our sakes, I thought I would try.

The first thing we did after Pamela instructed me on my morning makeup was go to the shopping mall to buy more clothes for me. In the lingerie department, she chose a padded bra. I felt foolish trying it on and even more silly when I gazed at my exaggerated figure in the mirror. I looked years older just with that cosmetic change and complained that I didn't look like the real me.

"That's exactly what I want for you," she insisted. "I know these contest judges. When you're in a Miss Teen this or that contest and you look older, they're impressed, especially the men."

I was still so surprised that she really believed I could be in any such contest. What did she see in my face that I couldn't see, that no one else saw? I thought I was plain-looking, even with the appearance of bigger breasts. Moving with the bra on reminded me of wearing a baseball catcher's chest protector. I felt bulky and thought everyone was looking at me because my bosom didn't fit the rest of me.

Before we left the store, she bought me a half dozen more skirt-and-blouse outfits, three more pairs of shoes to complete the out-fits, a necklace, three pairs of earrings, and a beautiful pinky ring — a gold band with a variety of baguettes. She then made an appointment for me to have my hair trimmed and styled by her beautician the day before she would enroll me at Agnes Fodor.

When we returned home, my charm lessons began, although she told me that every moment I spent with her would be like being in charm school. She was right.

As we rode in the limousine, she instructed me on how I was to sit. She demonstrated her posture, the way she held her head, and how she kept her legs either pressed tightly together or crossed properly.

"We're going to meet many different people over the next few days, Brooke. Whenever I introduce you to someone, don't say 'Hi.' I know young people today always use that, but you want to sound cultured. Always respond with 'Hello. I'm glad to meet you.' And always look at the person, have direct eye contact so the person feels you are paying attention to him or her and not looking over their shoulder at some gorgeous man. You can shake hands. It's proper, but you will be introduced to some of our European acquaintances as well, and they have the habit of kissing cheeks. For now, follow my lead. If I do it, you'll do it. First, put your right cheek to the right cheek of the person you're greeting, and then pull back slightly and do it again with your left cheek. Most of them like to do what is called air kissing."

"Air kissing?"

"Yes, you really don't press your lips to someone's face. You kiss the air, smacking your lips loudly enough to sound like a kiss. You'll get the hang of it," she promised with a smile.

It all sounded so silly to me. Actually, it reminded me of some of the rules Billy Tompson had come up with when I was ten and we were forming our secret club at the orphanage. He had a specially designed handshake that started with the pressing of thumbs, and he also had secret passwords. Maybe cultured, sophisticated people simply had their own club.

"I hate 'okays,' too, another big teenage word these days. When someone says, 'How are you?' you reply, 'Very well, thank you,' or 'Fine, thank you.'

"All this," she explained, "is really going to be important when the judges do their little interviews. They'll be judging you on poise and charm."

"What judges?"

"The contest judges. Aren't you listening?" she asked with irritation in her voice.

"I'm listening, but when will I be in a contest?"

"Well, of course, I don't want to enter you

in anything before you're ready, but I think in about six months," she replied.

"Six months! What contest is that?"

"It's not one of the most prestigious, but it's a good one to cut your teeth on," she said. "It's the Miss New York Teenage Tourist Pageant held in Albany. The winner gets awarded scholarship money, not that you need that, and represents the state in a number of advertising promotions, print displays, and even a video. I'd like you to win," she said firmly.

Win? I wouldn't have the nerve to set foot in the door, much less go up on a stage, but Pamela had that determined look on her face that I had already come to recognize, and when that look came over her, it was better not to contradict her.

My education in what I now thought of as Proper Behavior for Blue Bloods continued as soon as we arrived home each day. The first afternoon was set aside for table etiquette. Suddenly, the dining room became a classroom.

"Sit straight," she instructed, and demonstrated. "You can lean slightly against the back of the chair. Keep your hands in your lap when you're not actually eating so you don't fidget with silverware. I hate that, especially when people tap forks on plates or the table.

Rude, rude, rude. You may, as I'm doing now, rest your hand or your wrist on the table, but not your whole forearm. Don't, absolutely don't, put your hands through your hair. Hairs often float off and settle on dishes and food.

"If you have to lean forward to hear someone's conversation, you can put your elbows on the table. In fact, as you see when I do it, it looks more graceful than just leaning over stupidly. See?"

"Yes," I said, and then she made me do everything she had instructed.

"Teenagers," she said, again pronouncing the word as if we were primitive animals, "often tip their chairs back. Never do that. Of course, you know to put your napkin on your lap, but you should, out of courtesy, wait for the hostess to put hers there first. Since I'm the hostess of this house, at any of our dinners, wait for me. Understood?"

I nodded.

"Don't flap it out, either. I hate that. Some of Peter's friends wave their napkins so hard over their plates that they blow out the candle flames. They're so crude.

"Just like with the napkin," she said when Joline began serving our food, "you don't begin eating until the hostess begins.

"The first day you were here, you didn't

know which piece of silverware to use first. Always start with the implement of each type that is farthest from the plate.

"Now, watch how I cut my meat, how I use my fork, and how I chew my food. Don't cut too big a piece. Chew with your mouth closed, and never talk with food in your mouth. If someone asks you a question while you're chewing, finish chewing and then reply. If your dinner partner is sophisticated, they will know to wait.

"At Agnes Fodor, you will see that the girls follow these rules of etiquette, Brooke. I don't want you to feel inferior in the school dining room. If you make a mistake, don't dwell on it, understand?"

"Yes," I said. I was never so nervous eating. In fact, my nerves were so frazzled, the food bubbled in my stomach, and I didn't remember tasting anything.

At dinner, I was to perform for Peter's benefit. I shifted my eyes to Pamela after every move, almost after every bite, to see whether she was pleased or not. Usually, she nodded slightly or raised her eyebrows if something wasn't right.

"You're doing wonders with her," Peter declared. "I told you that you were in the hands of an expert when it comes to style and beauty, didn't I, Brooke?"

71

"Yes," I admitted.

"I almost didn't recognize this girl," he told Pamela. "Is this the same poor waif we brought home to be our new daughter?" he joked. "Pamela, you're a master at this."

Pamela gloated in the light of Peter's compliments. Afterward, when she and I were alone, she began what she considered the second stage of my development: how to handle men.

"Do you see how often Peter gives me a compliment?" she asked. I nodded, because I did, and I wondered if all husbands were like that. "Well, it doesn't happen by accident. If you let a man know that you expect him to show his appreciation, he will fall all over himself doing just that. I'm a professional woman," she explained. "I've made femininity my profession, and I don't mean I'm one of those women's liberation creatures you see in magazines and on television news complaining. They think they'll get what they want by demanding and protesting.

"There's only one sure way to get what you want from a man," she declared. "Make him think that you believe he is someone special and that you'll always treat him that way if he treats you as someone special. Make him believe he is your protector. Be fragile, dainty. You need his strength. He'll go mad trying to protect you, to keep you happy, and *voilà*," she said with a wide gesture, "you'll always get what you want.

"It's easier than protesting, and you enjoy yourself at the same time. Who wants to be marching with placards in the hot sun, screaming and burning bras? And who wants to look like that? Some of them wouldn't be caught dead wearing lipstick, even though they look so pale you'd think they were dead.

"I hope you understand what I'm saying, Brooke. It's very important."

I did and I didn't. Men and boys were still a big mystery to me. I felt more comfortable and secure standing up to them, since I was as strong as they were, as fast on the ball field, and never acted as if I were a weak sister. I knew they respected me, because they often chose me to be on their teams before they chose some of their male friends, but I realized this was not something Pamela would want to hear.

"Did you see the way I batted my eyelashes at Peter? Did you hear me laugh, and did you catch the movement of my eyes and shoulders? Observe me at all times," she instructed.

I was really shocked. Did Pamela actually plan every gesture, every turn of her shoulders, every movement of her eyes and mouth? And if she did, was that right? It seemed to me that she was conniving against Peter, fooling and manipulating him, and I wondered if that was something you did with someone you loved. I had to ask.

"But wouldn't Peter do anything for you, anyway, because he loves you?"

She laughed. "How do you think you get someone to love you, Brooke? You think it's like the movies or in those romance novels? You think someone looks at you like in that old song, across a crowded room, and thunderbolts strike? It's work getting someone to love you. And anyway, men don't know what they want half the time. You have to show them what they want.

"Most men think a beautiful woman is someone with big breasts whose hips swing like the pendulum in a grandfather's clock, but a beautiful woman is far more than that, Brooke. You have to nurture and develop your beauty, just as I'm showing you. And then," she said, pulling her shoulders back, "you will know, and all the men who look at you will know, you are special.

"When you're special," she concluded, "they all fall in love with you, and you have your pick of the crowd. That," she said, "is what happened to me and what will happen to you if you do what I say."

Was winning a man the only reason for our

existence and our only purpose for being? I wanted to ask, but like so many thoughts and questions tickling the tip of my tongue, I swallowed them back and stored them for some other time rather than risk her anger and disapproval.

Despite the way she talked and thought, I wanted her to love me as a mother. I wanted Peter to be my father. I wanted us to be a family. I wanted to laugh and have fun, to do things I saw other girls my age do with their families. It's only natural for Pamela to want me to be like her, I thought. That way, she would feel she really had a daughter.

What did surprise and even frighten me a bit, however, were her instructions to me on our way to enroll me at the Agnes Fodor school. She wanted to me to start my new life with a big lie.

"Except for Mrs. Harper, the principal, Brooke, I don't want anyone else to know you came from an orphanage."

"What? What do you mean?" I asked.

"Mrs. Harper understands why I would like it that way. Believe me," she said, "you will feel more comfortable, especially in the company of the other girls, if that little detail was forgotten."

Forgotten? Little detail? All my life, I'd been an orphan. I had no other experiences.

How could I pretend to be someone else?

"But what will I say?" I asked. "What will I tell people about myself?"

"Tell them you're our daughter. Tell them we decided to send you to Agnes Fodor because your public school has degenerated. A new group of lower-class students has gradually become the majority at the public school, and there was a lot of trouble. Your parents became concerned about your safety as well as your education. Most of the girls will understand, because most of them have had that experience. Their parents enrolled them in Agnes Fodor to get them away from inferior public education and bad influences.

"If you behave as I've been teaching you how to behave, everyone will believe you are who you say you are. At least, you won't be ashamed to invite them to your home, will you?" she asked. "I really don't think you'll have any problems," she added with a smile of confidence. "When in doubt, just keep silent until you confer with me.

"Or you can talk about me," she continued. "Tell them about my modeling, my titles. Most of their mothers are nowhere near as attractive, and they'll be jealous of you immediately."

She smiled. "I'm so excited for you. I remember when I first enrolled in charm school. I'm sure Peter and I will be very proud of you very soon," she added.

I looked out the car window. When I lived in the orphanage and I had nothing of any real value, not even a name, I didn't have to lie. Now that I was rich, now that I lived in a palace and had more clothes in my closet than ten girls all together had at the orphanage, now that I had servants and rode in a limousine, I had to pretend I was someone else.

The road to happiness was long and winding, full of traps and illusions. When I said good-bye to the girl I was when I lived at the orphanage, I never dreamed I would want her back, but for a moment, on our way to this wonderful new school for the rich and privileged, I longed to return to who I was, who I had been, just as you sometimes wish you could put on clothes that were comfortable, broken in, part of your personality, even if they were out of style and too old.

"There it is," Pamela declared. "Agnes Fodor. It doesn't even look like a school, does it?"

I gazed at the large cobblestone building set in a small valley and surrounded by greenery, beautiful trees, and a small pond in the rear. Everything was clean and perfect. And so quiet. She was right. It didn't look like a school. It looked like an old-age home.

I took a deep breath. What Pamela really should have taught me was acting. I was very uneasy. I didn't wear lies well. Surely, anyone who spoke to me would see right through my stories and answers, and then, then, it would be even worse. With a pounding heart and feet that felt as if they were plodding through mud, I entered the new school to become a new person.

5

A Shining Star

With suspicious, cold gray eyes, Mrs. Harper
stared across her desk at me. I was quite overwhelmed by the school. The lobby had a
mural that reached from the floor to the
ceiling. It was a painting of cherubs looking
up devoutly at a burning lamp. The marble
floors glistened around the sofas, chairs, and
tables. A girl of about fifteen greeted us as
soon as we entered. She introduced herself as
Hiliary Lindsey and told us she was on duty
as school receptionist. She carried herself,
spoke, and offered her hand to me just the
way Pamela had described and instructed me
to greet people. As Hiliary led us down the
corridor to Mrs. Harper's office, Pamela
shifted her eyes to me and gave me a nod and
smile as if to say, "That's how you are to
behave, see?"

I was even more nervous. The outer office
was as neat and spotless as the lobby. Mrs.
Harper's secretary, Miss Randall, was a short,

buxom, redhaired woman with strains of gray invading the hair at her temples and the hair at the top of her wide forehead, which formed rows of thick folds when she saw us enter.

Hiliary introduced us to her and then glanced at me to give me a small smile before she left us. Moments later, the inner office door opened, and Mrs. Harper asked us to come in. She was tall with very narrow hips and a small bosom barely visible under her loose, dark blue, ankle-length dress. I couldn't guess her age. Her hair was dark brown, her eyes hazel. She had a very pointed nose and a small mouth. Her cheeks were flat, which made her face seem more narrow, but she had the kind of skin and complexion I knew Pamela admired, not a wrinkle, not even a crease in her forehead.

Everything on her desk was organized, the dark mahogony looking as polished and clean as everything else I had seen so far. Before her on the desk was a folder with my name on it.

"Agnes Fodor," she began, with her eyes still fixed on me, "is a highly regarded, prestigious, and exceptional institution. My girls all have the highest-quality behavior. You will immediately notice vast differences between Agnes Fodor and your average public school," she said. Nothing in her face moved but her small, thin lips.

"For one thing, our classes are very small. We believe in giving the students personalized instruction," she added, turning to Pamela. "For another, our students are all on what we call the honor system. We don't expect our teachers to be concerned with behavioral problems. Everyone knows the rules we live under and respects them. If a girl violates a rule, she confesses her violation. Not that any do," she added quickly. "It is not unusual for a teacher to leave his or her classroom during the administration of an exam. Our girls don't cheat. You will notice that our lockers don't have locks on them. Our girls don't steal. You will notice that our bathrooms are spotless. There are no disgusting cigarette butts in the toilets and sinks. Our girls don't smoke in school, and most don't out of school, either."

"Smoking is the worst thing for your complexion," Pamela said.

Mrs. Harper looked at her almost as hard as she was looking at me for a moment and then turned back to me with a little bounce of her head on her neck. It bobbed like a puppet's head.

"You will notice that there are no pieces of paper, no refuse of any kind on the floors in our classrooms or in our hallways. Our girls don't litter. You will never find gum stuck under chairs. We don't permit the chewing of gum.

"After lunch in our cafeteria, there is very little for the custodian to do. Our girls clean up after themselves, and that even means wiping up the tables if need be.

"During the passing between classes, no one raises her voice. Our girls don't shout to each other. Never, never in the history of Agnes Fodor, has there been any sort of violent behavior. If two girls have a disagreement, they are encouraged to bring it to the judicial committee, which is made up of girls who are elected to the position. We have a very productive and active student government organization, and we have great faith in it. The girls police themselves. If anyone should violate one of our rules, she is brought before a committee of her peers and judged and punished accordingly."

"But I thought no one violated the rules," I said. I really just said it because I was a little confused, but Mrs. Harper's stone eyes suddenly became hot coals. Her face actually blanched, and the veins in her neck stretched until they were embossed under her skin.

"I meant they rarely violate the rules, so rarely that last year, the judicial committee met only twice," she said. "All year long.

"It is," she continued, turning to Pamela,

"very unusual for Agnes Fodor to admit a student who hasn't had a history of proper breeding, but given your and your husband's position in the community, we have confidence Brooke will quickly adapt to our high standards."

It started sounding like a compliment and ended up sounding like a threat, I thought. Pamela smiled.

"Oh we're sure of that," she replied.

"Very good," Mrs. Harper said, and opened my folder. She gazed at it a moment and then looked up at me again. "You haven't been exactly what we would call a good student. However, we usually find that our students experience an immediate improvement on their work here. We will expect no less from you, despite your unfortunate background.

"As your mother has requested," she continued, nodding at Pamela, "nothing about your past will leave this office. This folder remains in my files for my eyes only."

"Thank you," Pamela said.

"However," Mrs. Harper continued as if Pamela had not spoken, "you know that I know, and you know what I expect of you. Do you have any questions?"

I shook my head.

She stared, her eyes sweeping over me like

tiny spotlights searching for an imperfection. I squirmed in my chair under such intense observation. Finally, she closed my folder and stood up.

"Come with me," she ordered.

I rose and followed.

Pamela stepped up to touch my arm when I reached the door.

"Good luck," she said, smiling. I nodded and continued to follow Mrs. Harper. At the entrance to the principal's office, Mrs. Harper turned to Pamela.

"We'll be right back, Mrs. Thompson," she said, gazing at me and motioning for me to continue along with her.

She walked quickly, taking surprisingly long strides. I actually had to skip a step or two to catch up with her.

"This is Mr. Rudley's class, English. He'll be your homeroom teacher as well, so he has your schedule card," she explained as she opened the door.

Mr. Rudley, a tall man of about fifty with hair a shade darker than ash, looked up from the textbook in his hands. He was sitting on the edge of the front of his desk and jumped into a standing position as soon as he saw Mrs. Harper. The class, consisting of six girls, all turned and immediately stood. They gazed at me with interest.

"This is the new student I told you would be arriving today, Mr. Rudley," Mrs. Harper said. "Her name is Brooke Thompson."

"Very good, Mrs. Harper. Welcome, Brooke. You can sit right here," he said, nodding at an empty desk to his right.

I quickly crossed the room and waited to take my seat. Mrs. Harper remained in the doorway.

"I would take it as a personal favor if you girls would help Brooke feel at home at our school. She has transferred in from a public school," she added, turning down the corners of her mouth in obvious disapproval.

The girls looked at me. One of them, a thin blonde with blue eyes and freckles sprinkled over her cheekbones, stared at me the most intently. I couldn't quite tell if it was a look of welcome or of warning.

"You'll see to it that she receives her schedule card, Mr. Rudley," Mrs. Harper said before stepping out and closing the door.

There was a moment of silence. Mr. Rudley nodded, and we all sat down. Then he went to his desk and found my card.

"Let's introduce ourselves, girls," he said to the class. "Margaret?"

"I'm Margaret Wilson. Pleased to meet you."

Before I could respond, the shorter,

dark-haired girl behind her continued. "I'm Heather Harper, Mrs. Harper's niece," she added somewhat smugly.

"I'm Lisa Donald," said a girl with hair the color of rust and the greenest eyes I had ever seen. She looked older than everyone else because she had a bosom even fuller-looking than my fake one, as well as a more knowing, more sophisticated glint in her eyes.

"I'm Eva Jensen," a Scandinavian-looking blond girl said. Her face had hard, sharp features, and she was very thin.

"My name is Rosemary Gillian," said a girl with brown hair. She had a dimple in her cheek and a slightly cleft chin under thick, full lips. I thought she had an impish gleam in her eyes, especially the way she smiled at the other girls after she spoke.

"Helen Baldwin," said the girl who had first looked at me with great interest.

"Okay, that's it," Mr. Rudley said. He handed me a textbook. "I don't know what you did at your other school, but we're just starting *Romeo and Juliet.* Everyone reads a part. Some are reading two or three because there are only seven of us."

"Eight now," Rosemary pointed out.

"Exactly," Mr. Rudley said. "So, why don't you pick up the part of . . ."

"She can be Romeo," Heather Harper said.

"I'm not comfortable being a man."

"He's just a boy, remember?" Lisa Donald corrected. "Mr. Rudley told us."

"That's correct. Romeo and Juliet are meant to be not much older than you people," he said.

"And anyway, Mr. Rudley told us a boy played Juliet in Shakespeare's days," Lisa continued, "so who reads what part isn't important."

"I think it is," Heather insisted. "I'd rather read Juliet. Why don't you read Romeo, then? Why should you be the one reading Juliet?"

"Mr. Rudley told me to read it," Lisa countered.

"All right, girls. Brooke?"

"I don't mind reading Romeo," I said. I looked at the others. Heather had a smirk on her face.

"Fine. Then let's get back to the play," Mr. Rudley said.

When the bell rang, Eva Jensen and Helen Baldwin came over to me first and offered to show me around. I half expected we would have more students with us at my next class, but our group of seven stayed together for the remainder of the day. The passing between classes was just as Mrs. Harper had described: orderly and subdued. Other students were introduced to me, but there was little time until lunch for me to have any real conversations. Naturally, everyone wanted to know where I had gone to school and what it was like. Only Heather Harper looked as if she didn't think much of my answers.

"Do you have any brothers or sisters?" she asked.

"No."

"Are your parents very rich?" she followed. The other girls seemed to step back to let her take over the conversation.

"Yes," I said. "My father is a very important lawyer."

"So's mine," Heather said. "How rich are you?"

"I don't know," I said. "I mean, I don't know how much money we have, exactly."

"I do," she bragged, "but I don't tell people."

"So why did you ask her to tell you?" Eva Jensen said.

"Just to see if she would," Heather said. Then she laughed. "Anyway, I could find out if I wanted to. My aunt knows just how much money everyone has. Our parents had to fill out a financial statement to qualify for the school."

"She won't tell you," Rosemary Gillian said. "And if she knew you had even said such a thing, she'd throw you out herself."

Heather seemed to wither in her chair. "I'm just kidding. Everyone's just trying to impress you, Brooke," she accused, her eyes hot. "That's what they always do when a new girl comes. So what do you think of the place?" she followed, back to her cross-examiner's attitude.

"It's beautiful," I said. "I mean, I can't believe it's a school."

The others smiled.

"Neither can we," Heather said dryly.

"I'm glad you like it here," Eva said with warm eyes. "We can always use new friends."

"What do you mean, new friends?" Heather quipped. "You mean any friends, don't you?"

The others laughed. Eva looked as if she would cry.

"I need friends, yes. You can never have enough friends," I said, and looked at Heather. "Real friends, that is."

No one spoke a moment, and then Heather laughed. *Touché,* she said. "You know what that means?"

I wasn't sure, but I nodded. The bell rang, and we all rose. I saw how each girl made sure her place at the table was clean. I did the same and followed them out to our next class.

Heather came up beside me. "You don't

seem like you come from a rich family," she said.

"Why not?" I asked.

"You're too grateful," she replied, and smiled at what she thought was her own cleverness.

Everyone laughed, even Eva. They looked at me, and I thought, why not get right aboard their silly little ship? I laughed, too, and that made everyone, even Heather, feel better about me. Maybe I could do this, I thought. Maybe I could be someone I'm not.

Physical education class was the last class of the day for us. Our class was combined with four others that included ninth, tenth, and even eleventh graders. Altogether, we had enough for two softball teams. Our teacher, Mrs. Grossbard, was a former Olympic runner who had been on the team that won a bronze medal. She looked at me with interest when I came out in our school physical education uniform, a white blouse with the Agnes Fodor logo on the left breast and a pair of dark blue shorts. The school also provided us with sneakers and socks.

"You play this at your last school?" Mrs. Grossbard asked me.

"Yes, ma'am," I said.

"Call me coach," she said. "I have the wonderful distinction of being the school's soft-ball coach, swimming coach, relay coach, and basketball coach. I also have the distinction of never having a winning season in any of these sports, but," she said with a sigh, "I try. I do the best I can with girls who are afraid to break a fingernail." She looked at me. "Take shortstop on the blue team and bat fifth," she ordered.

I took the field with my team. Eva played first base, probably because of her height and reach. Heather was in the outfield, sitting on the grass immediately. The other girls were on the white team.

It felt so good being outdoors, stretching my limbs and using my muscles. We had a beautiful day for a softball game. The sky was a light blue with milk-white clouds splattered here and there. The light breeze on my face was refreshing. The sun was far enough behind the trees not to get in our eyes, and the scent of freshly cut grass was intoxicating.

Unfortunately, our pitcher had trouble reaching the plate. Her first three tosses bounced in front of the batter. Mrs. Grossbard told the pitcher to move closer, and she did so. Her next pitch was too high for anyone to reach, and the one after that nearly hit the batter.

"Wait a minute," Mrs. Grossbard said. She

put her hands over her eyes as if she didn't want to look at her class for a moment or as if she were speaking to herself and then took the ball and threw it at me. I caught it easily. "Throw it back," she ordered. I did. "Change places with Louise."

"Why?" Louise, our pitcher, whined.

"Oh, I don't know. I thought we'd try to get in more than one inning today," Mrs. Grossbard replied sarcastically.

Louise glared angrily at me as we passed each other.

"Warm up," Mrs. Grossbard ordered, and I threw in a half dozen pitches, all pretty much over the plate. "Play ball," she cried, her eyes brighter.

The first batter returned to the plate and swung at my first pitch. It was a blooper only about three feet in front of her. I rushed toward her and caught the ball at my waist. My team cheered. Mrs. Grossbard, who was leaning against the backstop, stood up.

The next batter took her place at the plate and struck out on three pitches. The third batter hit a dribbler down to third, and my third baseman, an eleventh grader named Stacey, made a fine pickup, which was followed by a throw good enough to beat the runner out at first base.

We went in to bat.

"You've pitched before?" Mrs. Grossbard asked me.

"Yes," I said.

"Why didn't you tell me that was your usual position?"

"I don't know," I replied.

"Usually, my girls don't hesitate to tell me what they *think* they're good at," she remarked. "Modesty here is as rare as poverty."

I wasn't sure what she meant, but I smiled and nodded and took my seat on the bench.

Our first batter hit a weak fly ball that fell just behind the shortstop, who happened to be Lisa Donald. She fell reaching for the ball, and we had a runner on base. Our second batter struck out, but our third batter hit a hard drive between first and second. We had girls on first and third when our cleanup hitter, a chunky girl named Cora Munsen, swung and hit a hard line drive right into the hands of the second baseman, who dropped it. We had the bases loaded, and I came to bat for the first time in my new school.

All eyes were on me, some hoping I would look foolish, most just curious. I saw Mrs. Grossbard's nod of approval at the way I held the bat and took my stance. My heart was pounding. I had to step out of the box for a moment to catch my breath, collect myself, and step back.

The first pitch was too low and the second too wide, but the third was slow and down the middle, my favorite pitch. I timed it just right and hit the ball hard. It rose and rose and went over the center fielder's head. The school's baseball field was bordered in the back by a small hill. The ball hit the crest of the hill and began to roll down, but it was so far away from the center fielder, she could never get a throw back to relay another before I had rounded the bases.

My first time up, I had hit a grand-slam home run.

And Mrs. Grossbard cheered as hard as anyone I had ever had cheer for me at my public school.

Afterward, everyone was talking about my hit. Girls were coming over to introduce themselves in the locker room, and by the time we all left the gym area to board our small, plush school buses, there was hardly a student at Agnes Fodor who hadn't heard about the longest home-run ball ever hit at the field. By the end of the day, talk about my hit was so exaggerated that the story going around school was that my home run had cleared the hill.

Mrs. Grossbard came out to speak to me

before I boarded the bus.

"Tomorrow," she said, "you sign up for the softball team, okay?"

"Sure," I said.

"Heck," she said, "we might even win a game."

Bursting with excitement, I hurried onto the bus, eager to brag to my new parents about my first day.

6

I Need to Be Me

Still filled with excitement, I charged up to the front door of my new house and entered, hardly able to contain myself. I was about to run up the stairs to my room to change my clothes, when Pamela stepped out of the living room.

"Good. You're home on time. Come right in here," she said, indicating the living room.

"I was just going to put my books away and change," I said. "I wanted to tell you all about . . ."

"Just step right in here now," she said with a firmer voice. "You can do that later. There is someone here I want you to meet immediately."

Obediently, I walked down the hall and entered the living room. A short, bald man with a face as round as a penny stood there gaping at me with big, watery gray eyes. He had a dark brown blotch on his otherwise shiny skull. It looked as if someone had splattered beef gravy on him because it spread in thin lines toward the back of his head and his temples.

"This is Professor Wertzman, Brooke. I've hired him to start you on piano lessons. Contestants need to show some talent, and the professor will teach you how to play well enough so you could perform something," she declared. It sounded more as if she had ordained it and it would be.

"But I don't have any musical talent. I never even tried to play the piano," I said weakly.

"That's because you never had one to play. What lessons were you ever offered at the orphanage?" she asked with a cold smile. "Now you have all the finer things in life at your beck and call. Professor Wertzman is a highly regarded piano instructor. It took a great deal to get him to free up some time for you, but he knows how important this is to me," she added, eyeing him with her icy glare.

When he smiled, his chin quivered and his nostrils went in and out like a rabbit's.

"It's an honor for me to be able to do you and Mr. Thompson a favor," he said.

"See? Everyone's trying to help you, Brooke. Beginning today, you'll have a lesson every day after school, so come right home," she commanded.

"But . . ."

"But what?" She looked at the professor, who widened his smile, and then they both looked at me.

"The coach, Mrs. Grossbard, asked me to join the school's softball team. I hit a home run in class today, a grand-slam home run my first time up at bat! I have to stay after school for practice every day."

For a moment, Pamela simply stared at me and blinked her eyes. The professor was uncomfortable standing in the long moment of silence. He cleared his throat and rocked on his heels with his hands behind his back.

"Have you any idea of the cost and the effort it took to get Professor Wertzman here?" she began softly. "Do you know that the professor tutors most of the pianists from finer families in our community? He has assured me he can get you ready to perform a piece in six months. No one else can make such a promise. You are a very lucky young lady." The way she said *lucky* made me think I was anything but.

"I don't care," I snapped. "I don't want to learn piano. I was never interested in piano. I hit a home run," I repeated, backing away. "I'm good at softball. I want to be on the team."

"Brooke!"

"No! You don't care about me at all, you just want to turn me into you!" I cried, and turned toward the stairway.

"You get right back here this instant. Brooke!"

I ran up the stairway and into my room, the tears flying from my cheeks. Then I sprawled on my bed and buried my face in my pillow.

She didn't have a right to do this, to make plans like this without asking me first. I don't care what she does, I thought. I don't care if she sends me back. I stopped sobbing, wiped my face, and sat hugging my knees, waiting for her to come angrily after me. I listened hard in anticipation of her footsteps in the hallway, but I heard nothing. Finally, I changed into what Pamela called a more casual outfit, a pair of slacks and a blouse that didn't make me feel any more comfortable than the clothes I wore to school. How I missed my jeans, T-shirts, and sweatshirts, I thought.

I was still afraid to go downstairs, so I opened my books and started my homework. It was nearly an hour and a half later when I heard a knock on my door. I hadn't heard any footsteps, and I never expected Pamela would knock. She always just walked right in.

"Yes?"

The door opened. It was Peter. He was

wearing one of his expensive-looking blue suits and looked as fresh and alert as he would if he had just begun his day.

"Mind if I come in?" he asked.

"No," I said.

He smiled and closed the door softly behind him. "So," he began, "it looks like we're having our first family crisis."

"I don't have any musical talent," I moaned.

"How do you know that?"

"I don't, but I don't want to play piano," I insisted.

"Well," he said calmly before sitting on the edge of my bed, "you're too young to really know what you want and don't want. It's like someone who's never tasted caviar saying, 'I don't want to eat caviar. I don't like it.' Right?" he asked in a soft, soothing voice.

"I suppose." I sniffled. I didn't want to start crying again, but I could feel hot tears building behind my eyes.

"Well, you don't know if you want to play piano until you try. You might find the experience wonderful, and you might make such progress so quickly, you'll get excited about it yourself," he reasoned. "You're a very intelligent young lady, Brooke. I'm sure you can understand my point."

I was silent a moment, and then I caught

my breath and turned to him, the tears still burning beneath my eyelids.

"I hit a home run in gym class today," I said. "It was a grand slam."

"Really?" he said, his eyes widening. "A grand slammer?"

"Uh-huh. And it was my first time at bat ever at the new school. The coach asked me to be on the team. She needs a pitcher, and I always used to be the pitcher at my old school," I told him.

"Is that right?"

"The team practices every day after school. The next game is only a week away. Every practice is important for me."

"I see. And you told Pamela this?" he asked, his eyebrows lifting as his eyes filled with concern.

"Yes."

"Now I understand," he said, nodding. He rose and walked to the window, paused there for a moment, and then turned and walked toward the door. "What if I could arrange for your piano lessons early in the evening after dinner? Do you think you could manage all that and your homework, too?"

"Yes," I said quickly, even though I had no idea if I could.

"It would only have to be this way until softball season ends," he explained, and I could tell he was still figuring out how to make it sound good to Pamela.

"But I thought the professor was doing us a favor and was only available after school," I said.

Peter winked. "We'll negotiate," he answered. "It's what I do for a living. The secret is never to panic but to step back, take a breath, and look for new doors through which you can enter the same house. This way, you get to be on the team, Pamela is satisfied that she is doing the best for you, and the professor is happier, too. I'll make sure of that. Sound good?"

I nodded. "Great. Then don't worry about it. Most of the time, we make our problems seem bigger than they are. When we look at them calmly, we realize that most of our dragons are created in our own imaginations. I want to hear more about that home run later," he said at the door. He gave me a big smile again and left.

I sighed with relief. I was lucky having someone like him for a father, I thought. No wonder he is so successful. He thinks of solutions and ideas so fast. He could probably even be president of the United States.

At dinnertime, however, I was still very nervous. Pamela sat with her lips firm, her back straight and stiff. I took my seat quietly, afraid to look at her, because when I did, she shot angry glances at me.

"Everything's arranged with Professor Wertzman," Peter said happily.

"I'm still owed an apology for poor behavior," Pamela muttered, her eyes lifting to focus on me. "Especially poor behavior in front of someone like Professor Wertzman. He goes from one important family home to another, and I wouldn't want him speaking poorly of us."

"He knows better than to do that, Pamela," Peter said.

"That's not the point."

"I'm sorry," I said. "I was just upset. It came as such a surprise."

"Here I am trying to do the best things for you," she whined, "and you make me look like a fool."

"I'm sorry," I said again.

"Everything's fine now," Peter said. "Let's just enjoy a great dinner and hear about Brooke's first day at Agnes Fodor."

"She could have had her first lesson today," Pamela said in a lower voice, retreating like a car engine puttering to a stop.

"She'll make up for it, I'm sure," Peter said. "Tell us about the school, Brooke."

I described my classes, teachers, and some of the students. Pamela was most interested in whom I was making friends with. She wanted to know about their families, but I didn't know much about anyone else's family, and I couldn't give her the information she wanted.

"You should ask more questions," she told me. "Show that you're interested in them. Even if you don't really listen," she added.

Peter laughed. "Pamela is an expert when it comes to small talk. Everyone wants to talk to her, but at the end of the evening, she can't tell me half of what they said. No one ever seems to catch on, though, so I suppose they don't mind," he concluded with a laugh.

Why wouldn't anyone mind if you didn't really listen? What kind of people were at these grand, important parties?

"Now, tell us about your home run," he finally said. Pamela smirked and started eating while I described the teams and my hit and the aftermath.

"Girls' sports are a much bigger thing than when you were her age, Pamela," Peter explained. Somehow, I think that just made her angry again.

"When they add tennis, golf, baseball, or basketball to the Miss America contest, tell me," she quipped. Peter laughed, but he stopped talking about it.

The days that followed were harder than I

ever imagined. There was so much school-work to catch up on besides the day-to-day work I had to do. Softball practice was the only thing I really looked forward to, and my enthusiasm put happy smiles on Coach Grossbard's face. However, it was physically demanding. Very quickly, Coach Grossbard determined that I would be the starting pitcher and bat cleanup. The only girl who seemed dissatisfied about it was Cora Munsen, who had been the team's cleanup hitter.

"You just had one lucky hit," she told me in the locker room. "You're not any better than I am at bat."

I didn't want her to hate me, so I agreed. "I'll do whatever the coach wants," I said. "It's the team that's important."

"Sure," she said. "Like you really care. You're just like the others. You want all the glory."

"That's not true, Cora."

She shook her head and walked away.

Most of the girls made fun of her because she was so big, but none of them ever said anything to her face. She looked as if she could sweep them off their feet with one swing of her heavy arms. I learned they had nicknamed her Cora Munching because she ate so much. She even sneaked food between classes. I thought that if she lost weight, she could be very pretty, but I was afraid to tell her.

After my softball practice, I had to hurry home to get ready for dinner and try to get in some homework. Occasionally, I didn't have time to shower before I sat for my piano lesson. Professor Wertzman didn't seem to care. He had a strange odor himself, an odor that nearly turned my stomach because he sat so close to me on the piano bench. I tried to turn away or hold my breath, but it was difficult not to inhale that stale, clammy, sour smell. I noticed he wore the same shirt all week, and by Friday, the collar would be yellowish brown where it touched his neck.

When he gave me instructions, he had a way of closing his eyes so that they became slits. Sometimes, when he got very excited about a mistake I had made, he would spray the piano with spit and then wipe it off with the sleeve of his left arm quickly. Often, Pamela came in to watch, and when she was in the room, his expression suddenly took on softness, his gentle, considerate teacher's voice returning. When we were alone, he spoke abruptly, had little patience, and complained continually about the difficulty he had turning a pebble into a pearl. It was always on the tip of my tongue to tell him I never asked him to perform any miracles, but I swallowed back my pride and let him lash me with ridicule and criticism.

One night, when Peter was sitting alone in the living room and reading, I stopped in to talk to him.

"I tasted caviar," I said, "and I hate it."

"What?" He looked at me, and then he smiled. "Oh. Right." He nodded.

"I'm never going to be good on the piano," I said. "Even the professor says my fingers aren't right. He says I'm too forceful and that I'd be better at drums or carpentry work."

"Is that what he said?" Peter laughed. "Well, just put up with it awhile longer until I get Pamela to think of something better."

"I don't want to be in beauty contests," I added.

"It can't hurt you to do it once or twice," he told me. "Look at it as a new experience."

"No one else at the school is going to be in any beauty contests, and there are girls in school who are really a lot prettier than I am. They're going to laugh at me and make fun of me," I warned him.

"Maybe you'll win. Then they won't laugh." The way he said it made me believe I really had a chance. Maybe Pamela *was* right about me.

"Will you and Pamela come to the home

game this Saturday?" I asked. I had been mentioning it all week, but Pamela pretended she didn't hear me.

"Sure," he said. He thought a moment. "I ought to get myself a video camera, too." He looked at me. "Don't expect me to become one of those crazy Little League parents, though."

I laughed.

When he brought up the game himself at dinner that evening, Pamela refused to go.

"Do you know what damage is done to your skin sitting out there under that horrible sunlight and letting all that dust come settling on you? When you come home," she said, turning to me, "you make sure you go right into a bathtub and clean all the pollution out of your pores and wash your hair."

She thought intently for a moment and then suddenly rose and came around the table.

"Let me see your hands," she ordered. I raised my palms, and she grabbed them and ran her fingers over them.

"Just as I thought," she said to Peter. "Her skin is getting rough. Soon she'll have calluses!"

"Really?" he asked. He sounded amused, and I could see he was trying not to smile.

"Come over here and feel them. Come on."

"I believe you."

"This is just ridiculous. A daughter with hands like a ditch digger. I want you to come up to my room after dinner. I have a hand lotion you'll have to use continually. You rub it in four or five times a day."

"Four times a day? You mean even while I'm at school?" I asked.

"Of course. How much longer will this baseball nonsense continue?" She was beginning to pout.

"We only have a few games left," I said. "I came on late in the season."

"Good," she muttered, and returned to her chair.

I was afraid to tell her that I had already agreed to try out for the girls' basketball team. The coach saw me shooting baskets with some seniors and asked me to come to tryouts next week. Besides that, Coach Grossbard believed I might get chosen for the all-star game this year and have to go to a special practice after the end of our softball season. Sports were the one thing I *knew* I was good at — and I didn't intend to give them up.

Peter decided that he would drive me to my game on Saturday. I was dressed in my uniform when I came bouncing down the stairs. Pamela was expecting her masseuse, but she was still downstairs giving Joline some instructions about a new juice drink that included herbs which she claimed retarded the aging process. As soon as she saw me come down the stairs, she began a stream of complaints.

"Is that their uniform? You're dressed like a boy. Why don't you wear a skirt, at least?"

"They can't wear skirts, Pamela," Peter said, laughing.

"Why not?"

"They might have to slide into base. They have to wear something practical."

"Why don't they wear some decent color combination, then?" she followed.

"These are the school colors," I explained.

"Whoever picked them out is not very creative. Remember what I said you're to do as soon as you come home," she told me, and continued up the stairs, mumbling under her breath.

"She's really very proud of you," Peter tried to assure me. "It's just that sports have never been important to her."

On the way to the game, he talked about his own interest in sports and how he followed football and tennis.

"I play a mean game of tennis," he bragged. "One of these days, I'll take you to the club, and we'll hit a few. Would you like that?"

"Yes," I said. "I've always wanted to play tennis, but we never had anyplace to play. My old school didn't have tennis courts, but Agnes Fodor does."

"Great. Now, that's a sport I might get Pamela interested in. She likes the outfits," he told me.

The outfits? I thought. They had the least to do with why I would want to play or watch a sport. I began to wonder if Pamela and I would ever understand each other. And wasn't that important? Having a mother who understood your dreams and desires, your hopes and wishes?

As Peter and I neared the school, I thought about the team we would play today — they were undefeated. The girls on their team did look tougher, stronger, and hungrier. Their leadoff hitter was a tall African-American girl who looked as if she could drive the ball through anyone in the infield. I saw how the girls on my team stepped back when I started to pitch, anticipating a line drive. However, I took advantage of her height and kept my pitches low. She went for two bad ones and missed, and the third was a foul that our first baseman was able to catch. My team cheered, and the nervousness they had come to the field with settled.

I grew stronger with every pitch. Once in a

while, I gazed at the bleachers and saw Peter smiling at me. He had brought his new video camera and was filming the game. I had three hits that day, one a triple with two girls on base. It drove in what was to be the winning run.

The other team looked stunned. My team gathered around me and cheered as if they had won the World Series. As we left the field, I heard the other coach ask Coach Grossbard where she had gotten the ringer.

Peter was really excited all the way home. "Wait until I play the tape for Pamela. That last hit of yours was a beaut, right between the right fielder and the center fielder. How'd you do it?"

"My coach at my last school showed me how to turn my feet to place the ball," I explained. Peter was very impressed, and for the first time since I had moved in with him and Pamela, I felt proud of myself and confident that they could be proud of me.

When we arrived home, Pamela was still soaking in her milk bath, something she did after every massage. Peter hurried in to tell her about the game. I showered, washed my hair, and changed. Peter wanted to take us to a fancy restaurant to celebrate. But first, he wanted to show Pamela some of the highlights from the game.

I waited downstairs in the family room. The two of them finally appeared, Pamela looking radiant and beautiful. Peter put the tape in the machine and turned on the television set.

"Did you wash your hair with that shampoo I bought you?" Pamela asked me — it was obvious she didn't care about how well I'd done in the game.

"Yes, I did."

She put her fingers through my hair and nodded. "You don't realize the damage the sun can do to your hair."

"I wore a hat," I said.

"It doesn't cover your whole head, does it?"

"Here she is. Watch this, Pamela!" Peter cried. It was when I had my first hit, a strong single to left.

She nodded. "Did you rub the skin lotion into your hands?"

I had forgotten, but I nodded. She narrowed her eyes with suspicion and felt my hands.

"They're very dry."

"Here's where she strikes out their best hitter. Watch these three pitches. Look at that."

"You should go up and rub in the lotion," she said.

"I will."

"Here it comes, Pamela, the triple. Watch this. There. Wow! That was the winning run."

"She's developing muscles," Pamela said with a grimace. "What girl her age has muscles? Sports will make you too masculine," she warned. "Why do you insist on pursuing these silly sports?"

I felt my heart sink. I had hoped that once she saw how good I was, she would not be so down on my participation in sports, but nothing Peter showed her on the tape seemed to impress her.

"I'm hungry, Peter," she whined.

"Fine. We're ready. So what do you think?" he asked. "We got a little Babe Ruth, huh?"

"I'd rather have a little Cindy Crawford," she quipped. "Hurry upstairs and do your hands, Brooke," she ordered.

I looked at Peter and then left the room. They were both waiting in the car when I returned.

"Watch your posture," Pamela complained from the car window as I approached. "You're hunching over too much. It's your shoulders. They're getting too big, probably from swinging that heavy stick of wood."

"It's called a bat," I muttered as I got in.

She shot me a fiery look of irritation and

then caught sight of herself reflected in the glass and worried about a redness in her right cheek all the way to the restaurant.

Not another word was said about my softball game.

For all she cared, I could have struck out every time at bat.

Even Mrs. Talbot back at the orphanage had been prouder of me.

Before dinner ended, I looked at Pamela and asked, "Did you ever play softball, Pamela?"

"Me? Of course not." She sniffed. "Hardly."

"Then how do you know you don't like it?" I followed.

"What?"

"It's like if you never tasted caviar but said you don't like it."

She looked at Peter. "Whatever is she saying?"

Peter smiled, but I didn't smile back. And then, for the first time, I saw a dark shadow in his eyes when he glanced at Pamela and then at me.

I looked away and thought about the wonderful feeling that had traveled through me when I connected at the plate and that ball went sailing. All the lotions, herbs, vitamins, and shampoos couldn't make me feel better about myself than I had at that moment. What would happen if Pamela made me stop playing? Would I ever feel good about myself again?

7

Trial by Fire

Despite my lack of enthusiasm and my dislike of Professor Wertzman, I was able to play a crude rendition of "When the Saints Come Marching In" five weeks after I had begun my lessons. Pamela thought this proved I was talented enough to perform at the first pageant. As the reality of my actually participating in that event grew, she decided to begin instructing me on how to do what she called the Runway Walk.

"The only difference is that instead of presenting some designer's new fashion, you're really presenting yourself," she explained.

We used the long downstairs corridor in our house, and she immediately criticized the size of my steps.

"You're plodding along like a robot, not walking. You've got to glide over that stage, float. Think of yourself as made of air. That's how I was taught. Soft, soft, feminine, soft," she chanted as I repeated the journey from the front door to the dining room. "Glide. Don't move your arms so much, relax. Open your hands. You can't walk out with your fists clenched! You're not smiling, Brooke. Smile. Stop!"

She thought a moment. "You can't look bored or uncomfortable, Brooke. Beauty must be ignited with enthusiasm. This is the motto I was taught, and you must learn and live it as well."

"I feel silly," I grumbled.

"You must get over that. What you're doing is not silly. It's professional. The judges must sense that you have self-confidence."

"But I don't belong in a beauty pageant. I'm not beautiful," I insisted.

She raised her eyes to the ceiling and looked as if she was counting to ten. "All right," she said in a softer voice. "Come with me now."

She walked briskly to the stairway and waited for me to catch up. Then she caught my hand in hers and took me up to her bedroom.

"Sit," she said, pointing at her vanity table. I did so. "Look at yourself in that mirror. What do you think are your worst features?"

"All of them," I moaned.

"Wrong. You have a great deal of raw beauty. Now, do as I say," she ordered, and pulled out her lip pencils. "Bold lips are back.

Not every young woman can wear bold eye shadow, but most can easily wear a bold lip color.

"If you knew anything about makeup and faces, you would know you don't have what we call bee-stung lips, so you should stay away from dark, matte shades. You need colors with more intensity. Dark colors will make your mouth look smaller. First, open your mouth." She demonstrated. "I want to line your lips fully."

I did what she said, and she began.

"Good," she said, stepping back and scrutinizing me. "I like to mix and match my lipsticks. In the morning, I'll begin with a matte lipstick. Then, later, rather than add more of that, which might look cakey, I'll smooth on either a clear gloss or lip balm. Sometimes I try a sheer moisturizing lipstick or colored gloss," she lectured as she worked.

She had my face turned to her so I didn't see everything she was doing, but she worked like an artist and then said, "There."

I turned and looked with surprise at my face. My lips were prominent now.

"My mouth looks so different," I said. She laughed.

"Audrey Hepburn, who had thin lips, used to outline just lightly over the lip line like that. Everyone has her own little tricks."

She studied my image in the mirror a moment. "You can wear a dark eye liner, I think," she said. She continued to make up my face, powdering, working on my eyes, until she had what she wanted and told me to look at myself again.

"Well?" she asked.

"I look so . . ."

"Pretty?"

I was afraid to use that word. Did I dare think it? "Different. Am I pretty?"

"I've been telling you that ever since I set eyes on you. Now that you are made up and see what you can look like, you should feel more comfortable and confident about yourself. I want you to do more in the way of makeup every day so you get used to it, Brooke."

"You mean put on makeup for school?"

"Of course. That's why I bought all this for you and had it here before you arrived. Every day from now on, I want you to prepare your face as if you were entering a beauty contest. That's what life is for us, anyway, a continually running beauty pageant."

"But none of the other girls wear makeup yet. They'll think I'm trying to look older and fit in with the older girls," I complained.

"Let them think what they want. They don't have half the beauty I . . . I mean *you* do.

Let's go," she said. "Back downstairs to practice the runway walk now."

She paraded me back and forth in the hallway for nearly another hour, using music, showing me how to turn, to pause, to look out at the audience, to make myself look seductive or innocent.

"Every contestant, every model, is really an actress, Brooke. You have to assume a persona. Think of yourself as someone special, and be that person for a while. Sometimes I imagined myself like Marilyn Monroe, and sometimes I was more subtle, an Ingrid Bergman or a Deborah Kerr. Nowadays, all the girls your age are trying to be like one of those dreadful Spice Girls, but you will be someone unique. You will be . . . me," she declared, and laughed. "Just keep studying me all the time, and it will come."

Pamela's words scared me — she really did want to make me into her, and my talents and wants just didn't matter. I didn't understand — why couldn't Pamela like me for me? And, if she wouldn't even like me, how would she ever come to love me?

The next day, I began to feel a little better when I realized at least the kids at school liked me for the real me. On the bus that morning, everyone wanted to sit next to me and talk about the game. In homeroom, Mr. Rudley, who admitted he had yet to attend a school sports event, said he heard he had better show up at the next softball game. The school had a star. I knew I was blushing all over. When I looked at the others, I saw Heather staring at me. She looked so furious, it made my heart thump.

At lunch, I received all sorts of invitations. I was asked to girls' houses, told about upcoming parties and events, and invited to join clubs. Lisa Donald, who was one of the school's best tennis players, volunteered to give me instructions at her family's tennis court.

"You could come over next weekend," she said. "I'm having a few friends over, including some boys from Brandon Pierce." I knew that was an all-boys school nearby.

"Whom do you know at Brandon Pierce?" Heather challenged.

"My cousin Harrison, who's bringing a friend. We might play doubles," she told me.

All the girls looked envious. I had to admit that I had never played tennis before, ever.

"Never? How come?" Heather demanded. "Don't your parents have a court?" She made a tennis court sound as common as a bathroom.

"Yes," I said.

"So?"

"I just never played."

"Why wouldn't you play if you had a court?" she countered, stepping forward to put her face right up to mine.

"What's the difference?" Lisa demanded. "She'll learn now with a good teacher, me."

The girls laughed, but Heather just stared at me with those small, beady eyes. Helen Baldwin pushed in front of her to ask me something about our social studies homework, and then Helen started to talk about Lisa's cousin Harrison.

"He's a sex maniac," she declared. Everyone paid attention after she blurted that. "Right, Lisa?"

"It's on his mind more than it is on other boys' minds, I guess. When we were both seven and eight, he only wanted to play doctor whenever he came over."

"Did you play?" Eva asked.

"No, but once he chased me all around the property trying to get me to take off my panties."

"I wouldn't mind him taking off mine," Rosemary said. The girls giggled.

"Yes, you would," Heather charged. "Stop trying to sound like a big shot."

"He's good-looking. You said so yourself, Heather. You said you wished he would look at you," Lisa told her.

"I did not. Liar."

"What *did* you say, then?" Lisa questioned.

Heather looked at the rest of us. "I said he was wasting his time with that Paula Dworkins, that's all," Heather insisted.

"I bet he'll like Brooke," Rosemary said. The girls turned to me.

"Why should he like me?" I asked.

"He likes anyone new for a day or so," she replied. "But once he sees you swing your bat, he'll fall head over heels in love," she added.

"Yeah, and with all that makeup you're wearing, you'll be an easy target," Heather sniped at me.

The girls cackled, Heather the loudest.

"She's joking," Lisa said, "but he does like girls who are into sports. I know. He told me." They grew quiet. "That's why you want to learn tennis quickly," she said. "I imagine it won't take you long."

"It seems very strange that your father would never teach you," Heather insisted. "Don't you get along with him?"

"Mind your own business," Helen said.

"Of course we get along," I said. "He's just very busy." I was glad to turn the conversation away from the awful makeup Pamela had made me wear that morning.

Heather smirked. "That's exactly what my father says every time I ask him to do something with me," she remarked.

"The only difference is that Brooke's father's not lying," Eva said, and the girls laughed hard again. I had to smile. Heather gazed at me. If her eyes could throw darts, I'd have been full of holes.

The rest of the week went smoothly. Everyone was more excited than ever at softball practice. I did well on two tests, and my teachers gave me compliments on my efforts. Mrs. Harper actually stopped me in the hall to tell me I was making a very good transition.

"Just stay on course," she told me. Her eyes were so fierce, it sounded like a warning. I thanked her and quickly moved on.

At home, I performed my piano lessons with an attitude of resignation. I had come to the conclusion it was something I had to do, like going to the bathroom. Professor Wertzman didn't think any better of my playing, but he didn't criticize and complain as much as he usually did.

Peter was away most of the week on a big case that took him to New York City. The conversations about school and other interesting things that were happening in the world disappeared from dinner. Pamela continued to use the meal as a classroom, developing my education in proper mealtime manners. She was impressed that I had been invited to Lisa Donald's house for lunch and tennis. On her own, she had found out that Lisa's father was one of the Donalds who owned the local department store.

"I just knew you would make friends with people of quality," she said.

What did that mean, people of quality? What gave one person higher quality than another? Was it just money? I hadn't found the girls at Agnes Fodor to be any nicer than the girls I knew at my public school. They had the same hangups, problems, worries, and complaints.

Despite Mrs. Harper's resounding flattery and compliments, I discovered that her girls, her perfect girls, were not so perfect after all. They were just more subtle, more sneaky about the things they did. When the teacher left the room, they cheated. They passed notes, and they smoked in the girls' room, but they did it by the window so they could blow the smoke outside. Afterward, they always flushed the butts down the toilet. As far as graffiti went, someone wrote "Brooke wears a jock strap" on my gym locker, and Coach Grossbard had to get the janitor to find some strong detergent to wash it off. No one told Mrs. Harper. It was as if she had to be protected from any news of wrongdoing so she could continue to believe her girls were perfect.

Peter returned from New York on Friday night, and Pamela had me do the runway walk for him. She made him sit in the high-back antique chair in the hallway and watch like a judge at a beauty contest. I half expected him to burst out laughing when I began, but the look that came over him was different — I'd never seen him look at me so intently before.

"Well?" Pamela asked as soon as I made my last turn.

"Amazing. You've done amazing work, Pamela. She looks . . . older."

"Of course she does. She's more mature, more sophisticated and confident. She's been invited to the Donalds' for lunch tomorrow," she told him.

I didn't think it was a very big deal, but she made me describe the invitation, Lisa's offer to teach me tennis, and the rich boys who were joining us for lunch and tennis. Peter wore this serious look on his face, but he gazed at me with amusement in his eyes.

"You don't have a game this Saturday?" he asked.

"It wouldn't matter if she did. She would still go to the Donalds'," Pamela interjected.

Of course I wouldn't, but I let her believe what she wanted.

"No. Our next game is at home the following Saturday," I told him. "Will you come?"

"I'll try," he said, withholding a promise. "The way this Jacobi matter is playing out, I don't know when I'll have free time this month. We thought they'd settle, but they've decided to play their hand, it seems."

Pamela didn't ask him to explain more. I realized that all the time I had been living with them, she never asked him about his work or showed any interest in any of his cases unless there was a client who interested her, and then she was more curious about the person than the case, anyway.

"What's the matter with Jacobi?" I asked.

"It's not what's the matter with him," he explained. "It's his matter, the case."

"Oh," I said, feeling stupid.

To make me feel better, he started to talk about the case, but Pamela interrupted to ask if he had gotten me the sponsor.

"What does that mean? Why do I need a sponsor?" I asked.

"For the beauty pageant. Each girl has to be sponsored, and not by her own family," Pamela said. "The company will pay all your expenses, not that we need them to. It's just the way it's done."

"Who would sponsor me?" I wondered aloud.

"A number of companies," she declared irritably. "Peter?"

"I'll talk to Gerry Lawson tomorrow. He already gave me a preliminary approval. Don't worry," he urged her, and she relaxed.

Was this really going to happen? Was I really going to participate in a beauty contest? Me? I felt as if something was in my chest tickling my heart with a feather, but I was afraid to utter the least bit of reluctance, as it would put Pamela into a horribly mean mood.

Saturday, Peter drove me to Lisa's home. Pamela stood over me at my vanity table to make sure I did my makeup right.

"Who knows who you'll meet?" she said.

Pamela came along with Peter and me so she could see the Donalds' house. It turned out to be even larger than ours, which I didn't think possible. They had more grounds, a bigger pool, a guest house, and two clay tennis courts. Pamela said the house was a Greek Revival, and she was envious of the recessed front door.

"I wanted that," she moaned. "We should redo our front."

"There's nothing wrong with our entrance, Pamela," Peter insisted. She pouted, but when I stepped out, she brightened up to warn me to behave myself and remember all the manners she had taught me.

"Especially when you eat," she called. I waved and hurried to the front door.

Lisa answered the bell herself. She was already in a tennis outfit.

"Good, you're a little early. Come on," she said before I could say hello. She took my hand and pulled me through the large house. I could only get glimpses of the large rooms, the expensive-looking furnishings and paintings. I did realize the decor was different from ours, more antique-looking.

We burst out a side door and headed for the tennis court. There was a machine set up on one side.

"What's that?"

"Daddy bought that for us to practice returning serves. You'll see," she said.

She gave me a racquet and told me it was one of the best. Then she showed me how to hold it and went through the motions of how to swing. She was so excited about teaching me.

"I never met anyone who had never even held a tennis racquet before," she declared, but she didn't cross-examine me as Heather would.

Despite practically growing up with a

tennis racquet in her hand, Lisa wasn't very good. It didn't take me long to master the basic motion, and after a dozen or so practice swings, I began to develop a passable serve. I didn't think I was hitting the ball that hard, but she had difficulty returning my serve. I quickly discovered that all I had to do was hit the ball to one side and then return it to the other a little harder to defeat her. I held back, because I saw she was getting annoyed.

"You're so damn athletic," she complained. Then she stopped and looked at me suspiciously. "Were you lying? Have you played tennis before?"

"No," I said, shaking my head. "I really never have."

"It does seem strange, especially now that I see how you play."

I realized that she wasn't going to believe me. "I really haven't played," I said. "Honest."

She accepted that, and anyway, there wasn't time to talk about it anymore. Harrison and his friend shouted to us from the front of the house and started down the lawn toward the tennis courts.

The girls at school had been right: Harrison was a very good-looking dark-haired boy. He was tall, with long, slender legs jutting out of a pair of milk white tennis shorts. He wore a white polo shirt with black trim on the sleeves and collar. As they drew closer, I saw Harrison had thick, dark eyebrows. His eyes were almost black and set in a narrow face with sharp cheekbones and a strong mouth. He wore an impish smile on those firm lips and carried himself with an arrogant air, just the way a boy who knew he was good-looking and rich would.

His partner was shorter, stout, and light-haired, with a round face and blue eyes. His bottom lip looked thicker than the top, and there was a softness in his cheeks and chin that made him look more childish than handsome.

"This is your Mickey Mantle?" Harrison asked with a laugh. His friend looked as if his face was made of putty and someone had stamped a smile on it.

"Brooke, my cousin Harrison," Lisa said.

"Hi," he said. "This is Brody Taylor. You know my cousin Lisa."

"Yes, I do," Brody said.

"Are you as good at tennis as you are at softball?" Harrison asked me.

"No. I just got my first lesson."

"From Lisa?" He laughed. "That's like the blind teaching the blind."

"Really?" Lisa looked at me and smiled. "Why don't we start with boys against girls?"

132

"It won't even be a contest," Harrison bragged.

"We'll chance it."

"What's the bet?"

"What do you want to bet?"

"Virginity?" he quipped.

Lisa turned beet red, and Brody laughed, a sort of sniffle laugh with the air being pushed out of his nose and his body shaking.

"You're still a virgin?" I countered. It was as if we were playing tennis with words.

This time, Harrison turned crimson. "Okay, let's bet twenty dollars," he suggested.

"Fine," Lisa replied.

"Twenty dollars! I don't have any money with me," I cried.

"Don't worry about it," Lisa said. "You could always pay me back in school if we should lose."

"What do you mean, if you should lose? You mean *when* you lose," Harrison said. Brody laughed again.

"I don't even know the rules," I whispered to Lisa.

"Just keep the ball within the inside lines," she advised. She turned to Harrison. "Why don't you two warm up, then?"

"We don't need a warmup, do we, Brody?"

He shrugged. Harrison removed his racquet from his case, and Brody did the same. They took their positions on the other side of the net.

"I'll serve first," Lisa told me.

My heart was thumping. Twenty dollars! They talked about it as if it were small change.

We began to play. Harrison was good, but Brody was slow. I saw the way he positioned himself and discovered quickly that he was usually off balance. There were things that were common to all sports: posture, poise, conditioning, and timing. All I had to do was return the ball at Brody with some speed, and he usually hit it out of bounds or into the net. As we won set after set, Harrison's temper flared. He directed his fury at Brody, which only made him play worse. When Lisa and I won, Harrison threw his racquet across the lawn.

"You lied," he said, pointing at Lisa.

"What?"

"You didn't just teach her how to play. No one just learns and hits the ball like that."

"I didn't lie!" Lisa screamed, her hands on her hips. "That's what she told me. Right, Brooke?"

"It's true," I said, but he didn't look any more satisfied. "Let's forget the money," I added.

"Who cares about the money?" he muttered. "Brody, give them twenty bucks," he ordered.

"All twenty? Why do I have to give them all of it?" he whined.

"Because you let a couple of girls from Agnes Fodor make us look like fools, that's why."

Brody dug into his pocket and came up with a wad of bills. He peeled off two tens and handed them to Lisa, who took the money with a fat smile on her face. She handed me a ten.

"I don't want it," I said.

"Because you lied, right?" Harrison shot at me.

"No, because I don't need money and because I played because I wanted to play for the fun of it."

"Right," he said. "Let's get something to eat," he told Lisa.

She couldn't stop smiling. Harrison retrieved his racquet, and we all went up to the house where a lunch had been set up for us. It looked lavish enough to be a wedding reception to me, but to them it was just another meal. There were so many choices — meats, breads, salads, and different potatoes.

"Where are your parents?" Harrison asked Lisa. We sat at a patio table that had a table-cloth on it. Servants moved inconspicuously around us, cleaning up dishes, arranging foods.

"Golf club," she said between bites.

The food was delicious. I tried to remember my mealtime etiquette, but I was too hungry and started to eat too fast.

"Starving or something?" Harrison asked me.

"I forgot to eat breakfast," I said, even though I hadn't. It was something Lisa or one of the other girls would say. He accepted it.

"What took you so long to get here?" he inquired.

"Pardon?" I looked at Lisa.

"He means attending Agnes Fodor."

"Oh. I don't know. I just . . . my parents just decided I belonged there," I said.

He stared at me and then smiled. "Those real?" he asked.

"What?" I asked.

"Those boobs, they real?"

"Harrison!" Lisa squealed.

"Just asking. Nothing wrong with asking, is there, Brody?"

Brody, who had his face buried in the lobster salad, looked up and shook his head. His cheeks bulged with food.

"Well?" Harrison pursued.

"It's none of your business," I said.

He laughed. "That usually means, no, right, Brody?"

Brody nodded emphatically.

"What is he, your puppet?" I shot at him.

Harrison laughed. "She's all right, Lisa. Better than those other snot noses you call your friends," he said. He leaned over the table toward me. "Maybe I'll invite you to my house for a little one-on-one."

"What?"

"Tennis." He sat back, smiling. "Or did you want to do something else?"

"I don't want to do anything with you," I said.

"What's the matter, worried about your virginity?" he quipped. Brody started to laugh.

"No," I said. "My reputation."

Brody paused and then laughed harder.

"Shut up," Harrison snapped at him.

Harrison turned and glared at me. "I don't ask every girl to my house," he said.

"That surprises me," I replied.

Brody had to bite down on his lip to stop another laugh. Harrison caught it out of the corner of his eyes.

"Want to go listen to some music?" Lisa asked, growing nervous. "Harrison?"

He turned to her, a look of annoyance on his face. "What for?" he asked. "I'm not interested in wasting any more of my time." He stood up. "Maybe I'll come watch you play your next ball game," he said to me.

"Fine."

"Don't strike out," he said with a self-satisfied smile, "or I'll have my puppet here laugh."

"I can't think of a better reason not to," I said, and looked at Brody, who wiped his mouth, thanked Lisa for the lunch, and ran off to catch up with Harrison.

We watched them in silence, and then Lisa turned to me.

"Wow," she said. "No one's ever put Harrison down like that. Most of my other girlfriends swoon over him." She tilted her head and looked at me curiously.

"What?" I asked.

"You're different," she said.

"What do you mean?" I asked, my heart knocking like a tiny hammer in my chest.

"I don't know. You're full of surprises, like when you hit that home run. But," she said, jumping up, "that's what I like about you. Come on. Let's go listen to music and talk."

I followed her into the house, feeling deceitful, feeling as if I really didn't belong, but I wasn't upset so much about lying to my new friends as I was about lying to myself.

The truth was, the only time I felt honest was when I was playing softball or some sport.

The real me couldn't be hidden.

Harrison would be disappointed. I wouldn't even come close to striking out.

8

Bases Loaded

We lost our next game, but not because I struck out or the other team got so many hits off me. Our team made too many errors, the big one being Cora Munsen's dropping of a fly ball with two on base. The way she looked at me afterward gave me the feeling she had done it on purpose just so I wouldn't look good. Coach Grossbard might have thought so, too. Afterward, in the locker room, she kept asking Cora why she dropped it.

"The sun wasn't in your eyes. You were in good position. What happened, Cora?"

"I don't know," Cora said, eyes down.

"Well, I don't understand. Anyone could have caught that ball," the coach insisted.

Cora was silent.

"Maybe she was too anxious," I said. "That's happened to me. I think about throwing the ball before I catch it."

It really didn't happen to me, but I'd seen it

140

happen enough times to other girls. Cora looked up quickly.

"Yes," she said, grateful for the suggestion. "I think that was it."

The coach still looked suspicious. "Let's be sure it doesn't happen against Westgate next Saturday. We've never come close to beating them, and they shut us out the last three times," Coach Grossbard said.

"It won't," Cora promised.

The coach put up posters with the words "Get Westgate" on the locker-room walls during the week. I soon realized there was a real rivalry between the two schools, and pressure began to mount toward Saturday. It was hard for me to keep my mind on my piano lessons and modeling lessons while doing my homework and attending practices.

During Wednesday's piano lesson, Professor Wertzman had a tantrum.

"You seem to have forgotten everything. Such mistakes are not made by someone who is supposedly practicing!" he accused.

He jumped up and paced at the piano, shaking his head and looking at me furiously.

"I'm sorry," I said. "I'm trying."

"No, you're not trying. I know when a student is trying. I made your mother promises, and you're making it impossible to keep them," he declared.

Tears clouded my eyes. I lowered my head and waited for his fury to die down.

"I'll be a laughingstock," he muttered. "I have a reputation to protect. My reputation is my livelihood!"

"I'm trying," I moaned. "I'll try harder. I promise."

He stared at me with a look that made me feel as if I wasn't fit even to be in his presence. My lips began to tremble. Just then, Pamela entered. Right after dinner, her beautician had come over to do a treatment on her hair that she said would make it look fuller and richer. It didn't look any different to me.

"What's going on in here?" she asked, her hands on her hips.

The professor looked at me and shook his head. "I must have the full cooperation and attention of my student if I am to succeed," he said, shifting his eyes toward me.

"Brooke, aren't you trying?"

"Yes," I said. "I am. I'm not as good as everyone thinks, that's all."

"Who thinks that?" the professor muttered. "You can't be any good if you don't practice and pay attention. You are not practicing enough," he insisted.

"I do practice. I do," I said.

"Are you saying she needs more practice?" Pamela asked.

"At the rate she is going, more practice is definitely needed. I would like to see her add at least another four hours a week," he prescribed.

It hit me like a tablespoon of castor oil or a whip across my back. "Four more hours! When could I do that?"

Pamela stared coldly at me. "I think," she began slowly, "considering the sacrifices and the expense Peter and I are undertaking for your benefit, you could at least find the time. She'll practice an additional four hours every Saturday from now on," she declared firmly.

The professor looked satisfied.

"I can't practice any more on Saturday, especially not this coming Saturday. It's the biggest game of the year!"

"Game?" the professor asked, looking at Pamela.

"Don't listen to anything she says, Professor Wertzman. Please, give her instructions on what you want her to practice and what you expect her to accomplish this coming Saturday."

She turned back to me, her eyes like cold stones. "I'm filling out the application for the pageant's first audition tonight, Brooke. You have to be ready for every event. No," she said as I went to speak. "I don't want to say another word about it."

"But Saturday is very important. Everyone's depending on me," I blurted despite her order.

She stared and then looked up at the ceiling as if she were in great emotional pain. Without looking at me, she continued, "If there is any further problem or if the professor complains to me again, I will call Mrs. Harper and tell her you are forbidden from being on any team, baseball, checkers, anything," she threatened, her eyes still on the ceiling. Then she pivoted on her high heels and went clip-clopping down the hallway.

The professor turned to me. "Turn the page," he ordered, "and begin again."

The tears in my eyes made the notes hazy. I sucked in my breath and tried to swallow down the lump that was stuck in my throat, but it clung like a wad of chewing gum. I could hardly breathe. Still, I did what the professor asked. It was more like torture now, his breath on my face, his groans and slaps on the piano, but I endured every moment, terrified that he would complain to Pamela again.

As soon as the lesson ended, I rose and ran from the room. I charged up the stairs, my feet pounding the steps so hard the beautiful stairway actually shook. When I got to my room, I slammed the door behind me and sat at my desk fuming. I was too angry to do any homework.

Minutes later, there was a knock.

"Come in," I called, and Peter opened the door.

"I saw you fly by the den and heard the house coming down over my head. What's today's crisis?"

"The professor thinks I'm doing terrible and wants me to add at least four more hours of practice. Pamela said I have to do it on Saturday, too, and I have the biggest game of the year on Saturday. She said if I made any more trouble, she would tell Mrs. Harper to keep me off all the teams. It's not fair!" I cried.

"That does sound severe," he agreed. Then he looked at me with his eyes brightening. "What about getting up earlier and practicing before you go to school?"

"Practicing isn't going to help me. I'm no good at piano," I moaned.

"If you do it, I'll make sure Pamela doesn't call Mrs. Harper," he said.

Another negotiation, I thought, another deal arranged by my lawyer foster father. I was getting up earlier now to do my makeup because Pamela wanted me to look beautiful. I might as well not go to sleep, I thought. But what choice did I have? A foster child who was soon to be legally adopted was like someone without any rights or even feelings. If I wanted parents and a home and a name, I had to be obedient. Pamela talked about my auditioning for the pageant, but what I was really doing was auditioning to be her daughter.

"Okay," I said. "I'll practice in the morning before breakfast, too."

"Great. Another crisis solved," he announced with a snap of his fingers, and went downstairs to tell Pamela how it would be.

Despite my enthusiasm and determination, my new busy schedule took its toll on me. It was most difficult during my morning classes. I felt as if I was dragging myself through the halls and plopping into my classroom seat like some old mop. Twice in English class, I actually dozed off for a few minutes, and Mr. Rudley had to step up to me and shake my shoulder after asking me a question. My eyes were open, but I hadn't heard him. I apologized, of course.

Somehow, I came to life at softball practice. Maybe it was being back in the fresh air. It was the third week in May now. The foliage was full, lush, and richly green. Two nights of rain during the week brought out the mayflies, however, and most of the girls were

146

complaining. The ground was soft, even damp in spots. We all looked grimy by the end of a practice, mud splattered on our uniforms, faces, and hands, our hair sweaty, bug bites on our arms and necks.

None of it mattered to me. I felt I was at home, but my teammates wanted Coach Grossbard to have the field sprayed and dried. Everywhere these rich, pampered girls went in life, they expected someone would change things cosmetically to please them or make things easier.

However, when I returned home that afternoon and Pamela saw the little red blotches on the back of my neck, she went into a hysterical fit. At first, she thought it was caused by something I might have been eating. She accused me of sneaking candy bars at school. Then she thought I might be having an allergic reaction to something and started for the telephone to call her dermatologist. When I told her it was just a few mayflies, she stopped and stared at me as if I was crazy.

"Mayflies? Mayflies. Bug bites! That's disgusting. Get upstairs and into the tub immediately. Don't you realize how this could play havoc with your complexion, and you with a pageant audition only weeks away?"

"The bites don't last long. Next time I'll wear some bug repellent," I said calmly. That only made her more furious.

"You don't just spray chemicals on your skin like that. Do you see me doing such a thing? I thought I told you to study me, be like me. Upstairs," she ordered, and followed me. She surprised me by directing me to her bathroom instead of mine. There, she made me strip and go into her steam room. She flicked a switch, and the steam began to pour out until I could no longer even see the door. I felt as if I was being cooked and screamed that I had had enough, but the steam kept coming. I found the doorknob and discovered I couldn't open it.

"Pamela?" I called. "It's too hot!"

The steam continued. I lay down on the floor, because that was the coolest place, and waited. Nearly ten minutes later, I heard the steam stop, and the door was opened.

"Out!" she cried.

I was dizzy and thought I might be sick, but still I stood there while she inspected my body.

"Good," she said.

"It was too hot in there."

"It has to be that way to get out the poisons. Now you need your bath."

Joline had been called to prepare it. After I got into the tub, Pamela began to scrub my skin with a stiff brush, making it redder in spots than the bug bites, I thought. She poured all sorts of different oils into the water and shampooed my hair with such vigor I thought my scalp would bleed.

I stepped out, exhausted, when she told me to, and I barely had the strength to wipe myself down. I was taking too long, and she yelled at me to hurry up.

"Blow dry your hair," she ordered. Before she wrapped the towel around me, she suddenly stared at my body with more interest than ever.

"What's wrong?" I asked.

She shook her head. "It's still happening. In fact, it's getting worse. You look too . . . masculine. You don't have any soft places. Even your breasts are like little puffs of muscle." She grimaced, twisting her mouth, her eyes filling with concern. "I want you to see my doctor."

"Doctor? Why?"

"I don't think you're developing right," she declared. "I'll make an appointment."

"I feel fine," I said.

"You don't look right to me. Maybe you need some feminine hormones. I don't know. Let the doctor decide," she said, and left me.

I was almost too weak to hold the hair dryer. When I'd dressed, I headed downstairs for dinner. The only way I could be more listless was to be asleep. Peter was away on another trip, and there was even a possibility he would not be back in time for the big game on Saturday. Pamela sat at the table and lectured me about the importance of protecting my skin.

"There is just so much makeup can do," she declared, "and some of these pageant judges get so close, they can see the smallest imperfections. Don't think that doesn't play a role in their decisions. It does. They see an ugly blemish on your neck, they'll drop you a place no matter how well you do in the other categories, especially the male judges." She stopped to take a breath and then continued with her criticism. "Why aren't you eating?"

"I lost my appetite because I was in the steam room too long," I said.

That threw her into a new tirade. "It's not the steam room. Removing poisons should make your body more efficient. It's that stupid softball, standing out there in the hot, destructive sunlight, letting yourself be feasted upon by bugs, filling your pores with dirt. And you're not using the hand cream enough," she added.

She stared at me, her fingers thumping the table as Joline moved as quietly and as quickly as she could around us, removing plates, straightening silverware, filling the water glass. I stared back at her. Not a hair was out of place. Her makeup was perfect. She looked ready for a professional photo shoot. It occurred to me that she made a bigger effort to look pretty than the effort most people made to do their jobs well.

Afterward, my piano lesson was grueling. Professor Wertzman seemed to sense my exhaustion as soon as I began. Instead of taking it easier on me, he made me do all my exercises repeatedly, finding fault with every-thing as usual. At one point, he became so annoyed, he actually slapped my left hand. He didn't hurt me, but it was so surprising and sharp, I felt an electric jolt in my heart and lost my breath for a moment.

"No, no, no," he said. "No, no, no. Again. Again!"

As usual, I was nearly in tears by the time the lesson ended. When I went up to my room, I just sat dazed and looked at my remaining homework. I didn't have the energy to open the book, much less begin the written work. I fell asleep at the desk and woke with a start when I heard my door open.

"What are you doing?" Pamela demanded.

I rubbed my eyes and looked at my open textbook. "Just finishing some math," I said.

"I want to check your skin," she said, and inspected my neck. "I'm calling Mrs. Harper in the morning and making a formal complaint about all this. They shouldn't be permitting you girls out there until those bugs are gone."

"No, please don't do that, Pamela. I'll keep my neck covered. I promise. There won't be any bites on me tomorrow. Please," I pleaded.

"Ridiculous," she said. "All of it. Beautiful girls exposing themselves to such damage. Sports are for boys. Their skin is tougher than ours. Their muscles are bigger."

"Lisa Donald and I beat her cousin Harrison and his friend at tennis the other day," I pointed out.

She stared at me again with that strange look in her eyes, a mixture of concern and bewilderment. "I have heard where some girls because of hormone deficiencies actually think like boys. I'm beginning to wonder if you have this medical condition. Instead of taking pride in beating them at tennis, you should be taking pride in the way they look at you, at how you attract and capture their attention," she lectured. "Your doctor's appointment is next Tuesday, after school, so make sure you come right home."

"I don't need to see a doctor," I complained.

"I'm your mother now, and I'm telling you

I want you to be checked by a doctor." She smiled cruelly. "I know you're not used to having someone care this much for you, Brooke, but that's what it means to have parents. You should be grateful and not rebellious. I'd like to hear a thank you once in a while instead of this constant stream of complaint. It's all because of your stupid involvement with that softball team."

"I'm grateful. I just don't understand why I have to see a doctor. I'm not sick or anything."

"Sometimes we go to see the doctor to prevent sickness. Don't you understand that? Well?"

"Yes," I said, taking a breath and looking at my textbook.

"Well, then?"

"Thank you, Pamela."

"That's better," she said. "Oh," she said at the door. "Peter called. He won't be home in time to attend the mosquito feasting this Saturday. You'll have to arrange for transportation. I'm going to my dermatologist for a special Saturday appointment. He has something brand-new, a breakthrough rejuvenating skin treatment he wants to show me. Good night," she added, and left.

I felt more dazed than tired now. My mind was reeling, all her statements, declarations, and ideas bouncing around like loose tennis balls. I knew I had done a poor job on my homework, and when it was returned to me a day later, I was given a failing grade.

"If you don't pull your grade average up on the next unit test," Mr. Sternberg told me in front of the rest of the class, "you might not be able to participate in extracurricular activities next year."

I knew that meant all sports.

My heart felt like a deflated balloon. I looked at some of the girls. All but Heather looked concerned for me. She was smiling, her green eyes of envy brightening like the tips of two candle flames. Even Cora Munsen felt sorry for me. After class, as we all left the room, she caught up with me in the hallway and whispered, "If you need any answers next Monday, just look at my paper."

She sped away as Rosemary Gillian stepped behind me to whisper, "If you need your social studies homework, you can copy mine during lunch."

I laughed to myself, remembering Mrs. Harper's introductory remarks.

Girls at Agnes Fodor don't cheat. They were the special girls, the cream of the crop, the sophisticated, privileged, and cultured girls from the best families.

Sorry, Mrs. Harper, I thought. The only

thing really special about Agnes Fodor's School for Girls were the lies woven into the fabric of the school's emblem.

9

Smile!

We had our biggest crowd attend the Saturday game. It couldn't have been a better day for a softball game. The sky was ice blue with an occasional cloud that looked like a puff of smoke. There was just enough of a cool breeze to keep everyone comfortable in the stands.

Because I had no ride, Rosemary had her brother David come by with her to pick me up. David did not attend a private school. I thought that was odd until he explained he had made friends with kids who attended public school and didn't want to leave them.

"I've got some friends over at Westgate, too," he told me soon after I got into the car. "They said there's more excitement about this game than some of the boys' games. For the first time in years, there might be a real contest."

As it turned out, that was an understatement. The girls at Westgate were stronger and more determined than any others we had played. It had become a question of honor for them to defend their school's string of victories against Agnes Fodor. How could anyone lose to a school full of spoiled, rich, bratty girls?

But our team was determined, too. Coach Grossbard gave a great pep talk.

"Everyone out there thinks you're all a bunch of namby-pambies. They'll expect you to crack under pressure and fall apart just as we have in the past, but there's a new spirit here, and each and every one of you has improved," she said, gazing my way. "I'm proud of you girls. Go out there and show them what you're really made of."

We cheered and took the field. I did my best pitching and kept them to a single hit through the first five innings. The problem was their pitcher, a tall, dark, brown-haired girl with a body so muscular that it would put Pamela into a faint. She threw bullets over the plate. I struck out twice. No one was able to get a hit. Cora managed a fly ball, but it floated right to their center fielder.

An error on our side put a girl on base for them at the top of the last inning. The next girl struck out, but the next hit was a short fly that fell between second base and our center fielder. Her throw managed to keep their runner on third. One of their better hitters came up. I took deep breaths and looked at the crowd. There was a hush of expectation. Some people looked as if they were holding their breath. I spotted Mr. Rudley in the stands. He smiled at me and held up his thumb. It would have been nice to see Peter there cheering me on, too, I thought.

My first pitch went wide, but my second was in the low portion of the strike zone, and the batter went after it and missed. She fouled off my next pitch. Then she hit a hard line drive right at me. I stood my ground and caught it even though it stung right through my glove. Instantly, I spun and threw the ball to first. Their runner had gone too far and couldn't get back in time. It was a double play.

Our fans roared. Parents, siblings, and friends were standing and cheering us as we came off the field. It was still anyone's game. Then our first batter struck out on three pitches, and our confidence began to fall. No one said it, but I could practically hear people thinking that we would be the ones who wore out first.

I was up fourth, but someone would have to get on base. Heather was up next. She struck out with her eyes closed, backing away from the plate so much she brought laughter and sarcasm from the other side.

"What's the matter, honey, you afraid you'll mess up your makeup?"

"Afraid you'll ruin your nose job?"

"Watch yourself. That ball's got your name on it: Chicken Girl."

Laughter rippled through the crowd in waves. Despite our good showing, they still saw us as a joke. I saw how my teammates were taking it to heart. If we didn't do something now, we would surely lose, I concluded.

Eva Jensen was next at bat. I stopped her on the way to the plate.

"She's pitching a little more inside. Just step back and try to hit it to right field," I suggested. She nodded and took her stance. The first pitch was too low, but the second was right where I expected it would be. Eva stepped back and swung. It was a solid hit that bounced hard in front of the first baseman. She misjudged it, and it went over her head and into right field. We had a runner on first.

I looked at Coach Grossbard, who had heard me give Eva the advice.

"She's smart," she said, referring to the pitcher, "but she's not going to give you anything good."

I nodded and went to the plate. Once again, a hush came over our fans. The pitcher tried to get me to go after two pitches that were low and away, but I held back. The next pitch was coming in perfectly over the outside corner. It was the sort of pitch that required strength to hit. I leaned to the right and came around, catching the ball just down from the top of the bat enough to get a solid connection.

It soared.

And soared over the left fielder's head, and it kept going, clearing the fence. I had hit a home run.

I had been to ball games at public school, especially exciting basketball games when the crowd's roar was so high and loud my ears rang. That was the way it was now. As I rounded the bases, our side was screaming so loud it actually made my ears hurt. Mr. Rudley had a big, wide grin on his face, and Coach Grossbard . . . Coach Grossbard had tears of joy streaming down her cheeks as I passed her between third and home plate.

Cora gave me a hug that nearly cracked my ribs. Everyone on the team was around me, Heather hanging on the perimeter with a plastic smile on her face. I couldn't remember when in my life I was more excited and proud of myself. The crowd was full of appreciation, but sadly, neither my new mother nor my new father had been there to see it. I was as alone as I had ever been, even now, even when I wanted parents so much it made my heart ache.

Lisa Donald announced a victory party at her house. Everyone on the team was invited, of course, even Coach Grossbard. It was to be a barbeque. When I returned home, I rushed into the house, hoping my invitation to Lisa's might get Pamela to see how important all this was to me and perhaps make her proud of my accomplishments finally.

Instead, I found her in a mad tizzy. Peter wasn't coming home as early as she had expected, and before I had a chance to tell her anything, she cried, "Everything's falling apart!"

"What's wrong?" I asked, standing in the entryway, holding my glove and the winning ball in my hand. Everyone on the team had signed it, Coach Grossbard's signature biggest of all. The date of the game was there as well.

"Your pageant audition has been confirmed, but how I could have forgotten the most important thing, I don't know. It's probably because of all the turmoil surrounding your piano lessons," she concluded, popping my bubble of excitement.

"What important thing?" I asked.

"Your pictures! Your photographs! Oh,

where is he? Where is he?" she cried toward the doorway.

"Who? Peter?"

"No, not Peter. The photographer. I told him to be here and get set up before you returned. I want the pictures taken in the atrium outside the living-room patio doors. Those flowers will provide a colorful background. It will just look more . . . royal and make you seem more of a princess. Well, why are you just standing there?" she screamed. "Go upstairs and get the grime out of your skin. Bathe, shampoo, and start on your makeup. We've got to be ready in an hour."

"Don't you want to know what happened at the game?" I asked.

"Game? What game? You mean the, what do you call it, softball game?"

"Yes. We won. I hit a home run in the last inning and won the game. It was like the World Series or something. There were a lot of people there, more than ever, teachers, too. I pitched great. There's a party to celebrate at Lisa Donald's house. Everyone on the team is coming. Our teachers and parents are invited, too."

"Who has time for that? Are you mad? This photo shoot will take hours. We can't submit just any pictures to the pageant judges. These have to be professional, photos taken the way a model takes them. Would you stop wasting time and go up and get ready. I'll be along to choose what you should wear. Of course, we'll have you wear more than one outfit. And the bathing suit I bought you last week. Go, go, go," she cried, waving at the stairway.

I gazed down at the softball. What was the point of showing it to her? She might have it thrown into the washing machine. I started up the stairway.

"Can we at least go to the party when we're finished?"

"We'll see," she said. "I can't be thinking about any of that right now. Joline! Joline!" she cried.

"Yes, ma'am."

"Get up there and draw her bath. Quickly."

"Yes, ma'am," Joline said, and hurried to the stairway. She passed me by and was in the bathroom, fixing my bath of oils before I even took off my uniform.

I just sat there, dazed. I was certainly in no mood to pose as a model for beauty pageant pictures. I had come home on a cloud and now felt as if I was being dragged by my hair to be propped up on some stage surrounded by strangers, gaping at me with numbers in their eyes.

Naturally, I wasn't moving fast enough for Pamela. When she came bursting into my room, I was just sitting at the vanity table to blow dry my hair.

"Aren't you ready yet?" she screamed. "You can run like the wind around those stupid bases at a ball game, but when it comes to getting ready for something really important, you're a turtle," she fired at me as she crossed the room to my closet.

"My ball game *is* really important," I insisted, pride flooding into my spine. She ignored me and rifled through the clothes hanging in my closet.

"I want something with color, and yet I want to make a simple statement of your beauty."

"I'm not beautiful," I muttered, mostly to myself.

She heard me, though, and whipped around. "Stop that! I don't want to hear that anymore. I told you, if you tell yourself you're not beautiful, you won't be. Attitude comes through. Why have I been working so hard with you, training you on how to sit, to walk, to talk, to hold your head, even to turn your eyes, if I didn't believe you were beautiful? Pictures don't lie, either, so you had better change your attitude before you go downstairs. I want to see that effervescence, life, youth, your eyes radiating with confidence. Stop staring at me!" she yelled. "Get your hair brushed and your makeup done!"

"Okay," I said.

"Don't say okay. Say yes. Don't you remember what I told you? Okay is too . . . inferior," she declared for lack of another term.

She pulled out what she wanted me to wear and then found my new bathing suit.

"The photographer has arrived. He's a highly regarded professional. He's setting up in the atrium right now. I'll discuss with him what you should wear first and then return. By the time I do, you should be ready to put on your dress. Understand?" she demanded.

"Yes, but if we do finish in time, can I go to the victory party? Please?"

"We'll see," she said, and stormed out of the room. I gazed at the clock. The team members and their families were just starting to arrive at Lisa's, and I was trapped at home. My only hope was to cooperate and get it done as fast as possible.

I was ready when Pamela returned. She told me to put on the light blue dress with the V-neck collar. She made sure my padded bra embellished my small bosom and then brought me a thin string of her own pearls to wear. After I was dressed, she stood me in front of the mirror and fixed my hair.

"You look flushed. I knew this would

happen. I knew you would get too much sun out on that ball field and ruin your complexion," she said, and made me sit while she adjusted my makeup until she was satisfied. It took almost a half hour.

"When is Peter coming home?" I asked on the way down.

"I don't remember," she said. "Later," she muttered. I was hoping he would arrive before the photo shoot ended and would agree to take me to the party.

The photographer was a pleasant young man with dark curly hair. His name was William Daniels. From the way Pamela had raved about him, I expected someone much older and more experienced. When William began, however, I saw that he really knew what he was doing. Every time Pamela made a suggestion, he calmly pointed out why it wouldn't work, why the lighting would be wrong, why my profile wouldn't be as complimented, or why the backdrop would lose its value.

William sensed how tense and unhappy I was immediately and did what he could to make me relax.

"Don't fight it," he whispered while he was adjusting my posture. "We'll get finished faster if you relax and just let it happen."

He was right, of course, and I stopped

wishing and hoping it would be over.

"Great, good. That's it," he kept saying. Pamela relaxed more, too.

I hurried upstairs to change my dress, but when I returned, Pamela didn't like the way my hair had lost its shape and made William wait while she brushed it again until it satisfied her.

We had been working nearly an hour and a half. I knew the party was in full swing at Lisa's by now, and I imagined they were all wondering when I would arrive. Heather was probably telling them that I wanted to make a special entrance and was being late deliberately. That was something she would do.

Pamela had even more problems with my bathing suit picture. As soon as I put on the suit, she groaned.

"Can't you stop those muscles from popping out in your legs?"

"I'm not doing anything," I said.

"Is there anything you can do?" she asked William.

He studied me a moment, adjusted my stance, and shook his head. "She's got a great little body, Mrs. Thompson. I don't see why you want to hide it."

"They'll think she's one of those women bodybuilders or something. Who wants an Amazon to be Miss America?" she snapped.

"Relax your arms," she told me.

I tried to stand as loosely as I could, but nothing I did satisfied her.

"They'll hate this shot," she muttered.

"Let's just see," William said. "I might be able to touch it up here and there."

"That'll work for pictures, but not when she's walking on the stage in the flesh," she moaned.

He stared at her, waiting.

"All right, all right. Do what you can," she said with a wave of her hand, and he began.

Finally, the photo shoot ended. I ran upstairs to change into a pair of slacks and a blouse. I was back before William had put away all his equipment.

"Can we go to the party now, Pamela?" I asked, barely containing my excitement.

"I have a horrible headache from all this tension and trouble," she said, shaking her head. "It would take me hours to get ready for any public appearance."

"But . . . everyone's expecting me. I promised I'd be there. Please," I begged.

"I can drop her off," William offered.

I looked at Pamela.

"Fine," she said tightly.

"Thank you, Pamela. Thank you," I cried, and actually helped William get his equipment loaded just so we would leave faster.

168

"What's the occasion for the party?" he asked me as we drove off.

I told him, and he smiled, very impressed. Why couldn't my parents be this way? I thought. He told me about himself, that he was married and had a pair of twin four-year-old girls.

"They're as cute as two peas in a pod," he said. "I'm always taking pictures of them, as you can imagine, but I wouldn't want them to be in any beauty pageants. They're even having pageants for five-year-olds these days, dressing them and putting makeup on them to make them look older. It's out of hand."

"I don't want to be in one, either," I muttered.

"I could tell," he said, smiling. "But, hey, if it wasn't for people like your mother, I wouldn't be making a good living," he added, and laughed.

Talking to him helped me relax. When he saw the Donalds' house, he whistled. "Don't you hang out with fancy people," he teased. "As they say, it's better to be born rich than born."

If he only knew the truth, I thought, and laughed to myself. I thanked him for the ride and stepped out of the car.

Being late did result in a big welcome for me. As soon as I was spotted, the party came to a hush, and then they all shouted my name and cheered. Everyone rushed over to congratulate me. Many of my teachers were there. Even Mrs. Harper was there and gave me a restrained look of approval. Lisa's cousin Harrison, speaking to me with respect in his voice, tried to get me to be nicer to him. My heart was too full of joy to dislike anyone. To me, this was the greatest day of my life, and this was the best party I would ever attend, maybe even better than my wedding. Nothing could put a dark cloud over this day, I thought.

I was wrong.

10

Sheer Satisfaction

I felt as if I was floating above the party and not really a part of it. Never in my life had so many people thought so highly of me. At my public school, there were many girls who were good at sports, and I was always seen as just one of those girls from the orphanage, which was something that diminished my achievements.

I couldn't help feeling special here. I lived in a house as big as or bigger than most of the other girls'. I wore clothing that was just as expensive as, if not more expensive than, theirs. No one could look down on me and lessen my achievements with the simple words, "One of them."

I knew I was letting my head get too big. Lisa's brother and his friends had me surrounded most of the time. I was still wearing what anyone else would probably call stage makeup. I imagined everyone thought I had doctored up my face just for the party. I was too embarrassed to tell my girlfriends about the beauty pageant, so I said nothing.

However, I saw the looks of envy on some of my classmates as the boys vied for position, tried to do me favors, get me food or something to drink, and then tried to impress me with their stories and jokes.

Soon after I arrived, Lisa and Eva pulled me away, and we joined the other girls in the house to giggle and talk about the boys. For the first time in my life, I felt like somebody in the eyes of my classmates. I could even put up with all of Pamela's demands just so I could keep this moment and this opportunity.

Later, shortly before the party was drawing to its conclusion, Heather stepped up beside me and leaned over to whisper. "I've got to talk to you," she said. "I have something very important to tell you that can't wait."

"Now?"

She nodded and walked away. Heather had been ignoring me most of the evening, so I was surprised at her urgency. I followed her until we were far enough from everyone to speak privately.

"What is it?" I said, gazing back at the party. I wished it could go on forever, the music, the lights, the great food and excitement.

"I just overheard my aunt talking about you," she said.

It was as if we were in a movie and suddenly the camera stopped and the picture began to melt on the screen. The party actually turned hazy as my eyes clouded with fear.

"What do you mean?" I asked in a breathy, thin voice.

"I know you're an orphan and your parents are not really your parents," she said. "You never even saw your real mother, and you don't have a real father. You know what they call someone without a father?"

I shook my head. "I don't want to hear it," I said.

She smiled coldly. "I just thought you should know that I know," she said, full of self-satisfaction. Her smile faded and was quickly replaced with a look of rage. "No wonder you play sports like a boy."

"What does that have to do with anything?"

She smirked as if I should know. "Just don't act like such a big shot around me," she warned, and walked away.

My heart was pounding. The me I imagined floating above the victory celebration slowly sank down to earth. With trembling legs, I rejoined the party, but I didn't really listen to anyone or hear the music. Every once in a while, I caught sight of Heather staring at me and smiling, her eyes full of satisfaction.

In fact, I was grateful when Peter arrived to take me home. He was introduced to people who immediately congratulated him on my achievements.

"I'm so sorry I missed the game," he told me as we started for the car. "From the way everyone was talking, you were really something. Didn't you tell Pamela? She didn't mention a word of it when I stepped into the house."

"I tried, but she was too concerned about my photographs. I almost missed the victory party," I complained.

"She just doesn't realize . . . I'll explain it to her," he promised. "Slugger," he added with a big smile. He sensed something wasn't right. "What's wrong?"

"I'm just tired, I guess," I told him. I desperately wanted to keep anything from spoiling this day and this night.

"No wonder. Catching up on schoolwork, keeping up, learning how to play piano, bringing the girls' softball team to victories . . . talk about an overachiever. I'm proud of you, Brooke. I really am," he said.

It made me feel better. Pamela was already in bed when we returned. He hurried up to tell her more about the ball game and make her understand. I went to bed, and when my head finally hit the pillow, I felt as if my body had turned to lead. I sank into a deep sleep and didn't wake up until the sunlight hit my face in the morning.

Peter received a phone call early in the morning that ruined his Sunday. Even before I went down to breakfast, he had to leave to go to his office. It made Pamela angry, and she was in a sulk. I spent my time catching up on studying for exams. I didn't get half as many phone calls as I had expected. Peter didn't get home until nearly dinner, and I could tell that there was still a lot of tension between him and Pamela. It was one of the quietest meals since I had arrived.

All of it caught up with me that night, and I fell asleep with my books in my lap. When I woke Monday morning, it was later than usual, so I had to skip my piano practice and I didn't spend half as much time on my makeup. Fortunately, Pamela was sleeping late and didn't get a chance to inspect me as she often did before I went off to school. She did, however, leave word with Peter to remind me that I had a doctor's appointment after school tomorrow. I told him I thought it was silly. There was nothing wrong with me.

"It doesn't hurt to get yourself a checkup," he said. "Think of it as that."

If there was a compromise in the wind, Peter would smell it, I thought. Anyway, at the moment, he was obviously avoiding any more arguments with Pamela.

I felt something different in the air soon after I attended homeroom. Everyone has to come down from a peak of excitement, I thought, and this was what it was like. We were back to our usual day of work. The victory was already fading into the past, and there were looming final exams to consider and new work to do.

I was late for lunch because I had remained after class to talk about a math problem. When I arrived in the cafeteria, I heard what seemed like a little hush in conversation, and when I looked at the girls, some of them dropped their eyes guiltily. Why? I wondered. I got my food and joined my new friends at the table.

"I thought Mr. Brazil was going to keep me right through lunch period," I said, laughing. "You know how slowly he talks." Eva smiled, but no one else did.

I started to eat and noticed everyone was being rather silent. "Is something wrong?" I asked.

No one replied. It was as if I wasn't even there. The bell rang to move on to class almost before I had finished my lunch.

Everyone started to move away.

I reached out and seized Lisa's wrist. "What's the matter with everyone today? They act like someone died," I said.

She gazed at the girls who were moving toward the door. "Someone did," she quipped.

"What does that mean? Who died?"

"Many of the girls think you're a phony," she replied coolly.

"A phony? Why?"

"Because you never told anyone you were adopted," she said.

"Oh," I said, looking at the back of Heather Harper's head. She was laughing loudly. "Well, why did I have to announce that?" I asked.

"You didn't have to announce it, but you didn't have to pretend you were someone you're not," she replied.

"Yes, I did," I snapped back at her. "Especially here, where everyone judges everyone by how much money her father makes or how big her parents' house is."

"That's not true."

"It is," I insisted.

Lisa glared at me. "You probably knew how to play tennis all along, too," she said. "You made me look stupid."

"What?"

She started away.

"I didn't know. How could I know? Do you think we had a tennis court at my orphanage?" I shouted at her. Some of the other girls looked back, but no one remained to walk to class with me.

Less than forty-eight hours ago, I thought, I was a school hero. Today, I'm a school pariah. Once, when I complained that some of the other kids at my school made me feel inferior, one of my counselors at the orphanage told me sometimes you're respected more because of the nature of the people who dislike you. She was right. If anything, I was angry at myself for trying too hard to be like these girls. No matter how much money Pamela and Peter had, how much money they spent on my clothes, how many pageants I would enter, how big our car and our house were, I would never be like these girls. I felt as if I was born and had lived in a different country. I practically spoke a different language.

I put my head down and went forward. I worked hard in my classes the rest of the day. I ignored everyone. Most of the other girls were polite, if not overly friendly, but even my teachers seemed different to me. Maybe it was my imagination. Maybe I was feeling sorry for myself. Suddenly, I had little to look forward to.

My dark, heavy mood was lifted from my shoulders when I went to physical education class. Coach Grossbard called me to her office before I dressed for gym. She was sitting behind her desk with a huge grin on her face.

"I just received a nice phone call a half hour ago and waited for you to attend class," she said.

What could this be? I wondered. Did she just find out I was an orphan, and that somehow made her happy?

"What does it have to do with me?" I asked.

"Everything," she said. "You were chosen by the league to be on the all-star team for the county's all-star game. In fact, you're probably going to be the starting pitcher."

"Really? All-stars?"

She nodded. "I never had a pupil make an all-star team before. Congratulations, Brooke," she said, rising. Instead of shaking my hand, she hugged me.

I couldn't help crying.

"Hey, this is supposed to be a happy occasion," she said, laughing, but there was just too much emotional baggage for me to carry. I bawled harder. "What's wrong, honey?" she asked, making me sit.

I told her as quickly as I could. She sat back

and listened, her face turning red with anger. "They should call this place Agnes Fodor's School for Snobs," she said. "You must not let them get you down. They're all just jealous, that's all."

"No, they're not," I said. "There's nothing to be jealous about. They have real families."

"You're twice the person any of them are, honey. Real families or not. People are going to judge you for yourself and not because of your family name. You'll see," she promised. "If you don't feel like dressing for class today, you can skip it," she said. "Just rest up."

"No," I said, brushing the tears from my cheeks and taking a deep breath. "I'll be all right."

She smiled. "All-star. Wow!" she said.

It did buoy me, and I felt much stronger when I left the building than when I had entered. The word hadn't gotten out about me yet, but I didn't think my new so-called friends would be as happy about it as they would have been a few days ago. I tried not to think about it.

Pamela wasn't home when I returned. I went to my room and started on my homework, but my excitement was so great I couldn't concentrate very well. Finally, I heard footsteps on the stairway and stepped out to see Joline coming up, her arms loaded with packages. Pamela followed soon after.

"I had to get myself some new things to wear to the pageant," she told me when she paused in the hallway. "It's important that I stay in fashion, too. They take pictures of the mothers and daughters."

"I have something to tell you," I said. I knew how important it had been to her that no one knew the truth about me. "The girls have found out about me. They know I'm a foster child in the process of being adopted."

"What? How could that happen?"

"Heather Harper overheard her aunt talking to someone and told everyone," I said. "They're a bunch of snobs. I hate them. I hate that school, except for Coach Grossbard. Even the teachers are looking at me differently," I wailed.

She stared, furious. "Wait until I tell Peter. We'll sue her for being a gossip," she declared.

"What good will that do me?" I asked, but she didn't reply. She turned and charged back down the stairway. A little over an hour later, Peter came home. I heard their raised voices below and went down to find them in the den. Peter looked overwrought, his face flushed, his hair disheveled.

"There's no ground on which to sue anyone," he told me as soon as I entered.

"I don't want you to do that, Peter. It wouldn't help," I said.

"She's right, Pamela. Let's forget about it."

"I won't forget about it. That woman is going to get a piece of my mind. I'll speak to the trustees. She should be fired for doing this."

"It's over and done with," Peter said.

"I don't want to go there next year," I said.

Pamela looked up sharply. "What do you mean? Where would you go, a public school?" she asked, her lips twisted.

"I don't care. I hate those girls. And soon they're going to be even more jealous of me," I added.

Peter raised his eyebrows. "And why is that?"

"I've been selected to be on the county's all-star team. I'm going to be the starting pitcher in the game," I told him.

He beamed a wide grin. "Brooke, that's fantastic! I'm so proud of you!" He stood up and hugged me.

"What kind of an accomplishment is that?" Pamela muttered.

"It's the biggest, most important thing that's ever happened to me," I said.

She smirked and shook her head. "I can't take all this tension. It's bad for my complexion," she complained. She stood. "I need

182

to sit in my electric massage chair before dinner."

"Well, I'm thrilled for you, honey. When is the game?" Peter asked.

I told him, and Pamela stopped walking out. She turned and looked at me. "What did you say? When is that silly event?"

I repeated the date.

"You can't go to that," she said. "Don't you realize what that date is? Have I been talking to myself for weeks and weeks? That's the date of your audition for the pageant. It's all arranged."

"No," I said, shaking my head. I looked at Peter, but he looked worried. Surely, he would come up with one of his ingenious compromises, I thought. "I've been selected from all the girls in all the schools. It's a great honor."

"That's no honor," Pamela declared. "How can you compare throwing a softball to winning a pageant?"

"I don't care. I'm playing. I've been chosen. I'm not going to the pageant."

"You absolutely are," she said. "I'm going to the phone immediately and call that big-mouth principal. I'll tell her that I absolutely forbid your participation, and if she doesn't obey me, I'll warn her that I'm going to the trustees about her gossiping."

183

"Pamela," Peter said softly.

"What? You're not thinking of permitting her to go to the ball game instead of the pageant, are you? Look at all I've been doing, what we've spent, the piano lessons, the work, the pictures!"

"Maybe we can get her a different audition," he said, still speaking softly.

"You know we can't do that. You know how hard it was to arrange for this." She turned to me. "You're going to the pageant. Forget about that ball game. You're a girl. You're a beautiful young woman. You're not some . . . some Amazon. I won't have it!" she screamed. "I'm Pamela Thompson. My daughter is going to be a pageant winner."

"No, I'm not. I'm not," I yelled back at her, and ran out of the den.

"I'm calling Mrs. Harper right now," she screamed at me as I charged up the stairway. "I'm calling her! You can put that game out of your mind, Brooke. Do you hear me?"

I slammed my door closed and locked it. Then I threw myself on my bed and buried my face in my pillow until I couldn't breathe.

Why did this have to happen to me?

I sat up and stared at my image in the vanity table mirror. Why was I born if I was to suffer like this? Why did people have children they didn't want?

When Pamela came to the orphanage and saw me, she didn't see me. She saw herself. She saw what she wanted me to be, and then she brought me here and tried to make me into the girl she had seen. I'm not that girl. I'll never be that girl, I told my image in the mirror.

The makeup I had been wearing had streaked under my tears. I wiped the lipstick off and then, in a rage, went into the bathroom and washed my face until my skin burned. Afterward, I came out and looked at myself again. I practically ripped off my blouse and tore away the padded bra. I rifled through my drawers until I found the faded pink ribbon my mother had left with me, and I tied up my hair. Then I put on my blouse again and sat fuming.

I heard footsteps outside my door.

"Why is this door locked?" Pamela cried.

"I don't want to talk to anyone," I said.

"I just got off the phone with Mrs. Harper. You can forget that game. It's all taken care of. Now, stop this nonsense immediately. I want to talk to you about the audition. I have other things to explain."

The tears streaked down my cheeks again. My shoulders felt so heavy.

Everyone looked down on me at the school, and now I was losing the one big accomplishment I had achieved. Coach Grossbard would be so disappointed, too.

"Brooke! Do you hear me?"

I felt something shatter inside me. It was as if my body was made of glass and the glass had cracked. Soon, I would just crumble to the floor, and when she did come in, she would only find a pile of broken pieces.

"Brooke!"

The more she yelled, the more I felt as if I was coming apart. I reached out and seized the scissors in front of me, and then, taking fistfuls of my hair into my hand, I began to hack away at the strands, dropping clumps of it on the table, cutting and snipping away above the old, faded ribbon, slicing my hair without design until I could even see my scalp showing in places.

Pamela was pounding on the door, screaming my name, threatening, lecturing. I could hear Peter behind her, pleading, asking her to calm down.

When I was finished, I laid the scissors down softly on the table, rose, and quietly, like a shadow, floated across the room to the door. I unlocked it and then opened it.

When she saw me, her eyes nearly exploded. Her mouth opened and closed without a sound at first, and then she put her hands against her own temples and screamed louder than I could ever imagine myself screaming. Her effort turned her face blood red, and her body shook violently, denying what she saw, refusing to believe.

Peter stepped around her to look at me and fell into shock himself.

Pamela's eyes went into the top of her head. She threw her hands toward the ceiling and collapsed into his arms.

I closed the door softly.

Epilogue

"It's better for you," Peter said.

The grandfather clock's ticking seemed so much louder.

Peter sat across from me in the plush living room, his hands clasped as he leaned toward me. He looked very tired, his perennial tan had faded, and his hair was slightly messed up. He wore no tie. His collar was open and his brown sports jacket undone. I almost felt sorrier for him than I did for myself. I knew how bad a time he was having with Pamela. A parade of doctors and health-related people had come through the house, marching up the stairs to her room to give her massages, skin and hair treatments, nutritional guidance. There was even a meditation specialist who spent hours with her. She claimed I had aged her years in minutes and it would take months to cure the degeneration. She even complained of heart trouble.

I had yet to say another word to her or she to me.

"No one wants to make you live where you're uncomfortable," Peter continued. "Or go to school where you're unhappy," he added.

I looked at him, and he had to look away.

People who lie to themselves have a hard time looking at other people directly. They are afraid that their eyes will reveal the self-deceptions.

After my tantrum, Peter wanted to take me to a doctor, too. I refused. Actually, I felt fine, even somewhat stronger. It was as if I had thrown a weight off my shoulders. I had been trying to fit myself into a mold that simply did not fit. What I wished at this moment was that I had my old clothes back. I still wore my old ribbon around my head. I wouldn't take it off.

Peter sat back thoughtfully. The clock ticked.

Sacket appeared in the doorway. "The car has arrived for Miss Brooke, Mr. Thompson. Should I begin to load the trunk?"

"Yes, please, Sacket," Peter said.

I had told him that I didn't want my new things, but Peter insisted I take them. "What you do with them afterward is your business, Brooke, but they are yours."

I was adamant about not taking a single

tube of lipstick. The way I felt, I didn't know whether I would ever put on any makeup again.

"Are you all right to travel?" Peter asked me.

I nearly laughed. I looked away and then stood up. He had hired a limousine to take me to the foster home. All I knew was it was a group foster home run by a couple who used to run it as a tourist house. Supposedly, there were at least a dozen children of various ages already there. Peter was told, and he tried to convince me, that it was only a temporary situation. Other, more personalized homes were being sought, and I would soon have another set of foster parents, maybe even adoptive parents.

I couldn't help thinking about my mother and dreaming that she was the one waiting for me outside. She had heard about my situation, and she had come from wherever she lived to claim me. Now she was waiting outside in her car, and in a moment I would set eyes on her for the first time.

It was a wonderful fantasy, one that helped me walk with determination and confidence, something Pamela would be proud to see, I thought. That brought a smile to my face and confused Peter, who watched me with a strange half-smile of his own.

"I've arranged for you to have some money," he told me at the door. "It's been deposited in the bank."

I almost said, "I earned it," but instead held my tongue and stepped outside. It was a gray, overcast day with a stiff breeze that lifted the remaining strands of my hair from my forehead. It had been Peter's idea to buy me a baseball cap. I put it on.

He had spared no expense on the limousine, I thought. It was a long, sleek black car with a driver in uniform. He stepped out and waited.

"You're an exceptional young lady, Brooke," Peter said. "Don't let anyone try to convince you otherwise. Whatever you set your mind on doing, I'm sure you'll do. Maybe you'll become a lawyer someday and come to my firm."

"I don't think so," I said.

It wiped the smile from his face. He looked sad enough to cry. "I wanted better things for you," he said. "I hope you believe that."

I nodded. Then I looked back toward the stairway. Pamela wouldn't even know I'd left, I thought. What did it matter? We had never really become mother and daughter, not in the way I had dreamed we would.

Peter leaned forward to kiss me on the forehead. "Good-bye, Brooke," he said. "Good luck."

"Thanks," I muttered, and walked down to the car. When I looked back, Peter was still standing in the doorway. The breeze lifted his hair. He raised his hand, and then, as if hearing himself paged, he turned quickly and went back inside.

We drove off. The driver tried to make conversation, but I wouldn't answer any questions, and soon I was riding in silence, listening to my own thoughts. A little less than two hours later, we pulled up in front of the group foster home, a place named the Lakewood House. It was a very large two-story house of gray clapboard with a wraparound porch. I realized it was very quiet because all of the children were probably at school. The driver began to unload my luggage just as a tall man with dark hair that fell over his forehead came around the corner. He had a pickax over his shoulder and his shirt off. His shoulders were thick with muscle, as were his long arms. His hands looked like steel vises. The fingers easily held the tool when he paused to swing it down.

"Louise!" he shouted. He stared at me. "Louise!" he screamed again, this time followed with striking the side of the building with the flat side of the pickax. I imagined it must have shaken the building and everything inside.

Suddenly, the front door opened, and a tall brunette with shoulder-length hair came hurrying out. She looked about fifty, with soft wrinkles on the sides of her eyes and over her upper lip, wrinkles that would have given Pamela the heart attack she claimed I had almost given her. Louise had young, vibrant-looking, friendly blue eyes, however.

"Sure she brought enough?" the big man asked, nodding at my pile of suitcases and bags.

"We'll find a place for everything," Louise assured me.

"Not in the room she has," he corrected.

"We'll figure it out. Hi, honey. My name's Louise. This is my husband, Gordon. He looks after the place. Did you have a long ride?"

"No," I said.

"She wouldn't feel a long ride in a car like that, anyway," Gordon said, drawing closer. He stood gazing at me as he wiped his hands on his pants.

"You're lucky. You have your own room. You don't need to share at the moment, but Gordon's right. There's not enough closet space for all this," Louise said, looking at the luggage.

The driver slammed the trunk.

"What'd ya get for something like this?" Gordon asked him.

"A hundred and fifty," the driver answered quietly.

"Maybe I oughtta go into the limo business," Gordon muttered.

"Be my guest," the driver said, and got into the car. We didn't say good-bye since we never really said hello. I didn't even know his name, and I doubted if he knew mine.

"Who's supposed to carry all this inside?" Gordon asked.

"I can do it myself," I said. "Don't worry about space. There's a lot I don't want."

He stared at me with a sharpness and then smiled. "Independent, huh?" he asked.

"Let's get her settled in first, Gordon. Then we'll all get to know each other."

"Can't wait," Gordon said, and sauntered off toward the garage.

"Gordon's not used to having children around the house," Louise explained. "We ran this as a prime tourist resort. But that was before the resort business began to suffer," she continued, and explained her history and the building's as we took in some of my things and I settled in my room. Then she showed me around the house, where the dining room was, the game room, the kitchen, explaining what went on in each during the heyday of the resort period. There were pictures on the walls of guests and employees. I did think it was interesting and almost felt as if I had come to a hotel.

But that was a feeling that wouldn't last long.

"I'll get you into school tomorrow," Louise promised. "For now, why don't you rest and wait for the others to come home? You'll make lots of friends here," she predicted.

I didn't say anything. The overcast sky was beginning to break up so that patches of blue were visible here and there. The breeze was still strong but warm. I walked the grounds and sat at the top of a small hill, looking down at the lake. There were interesting, beautiful birds to watch. I was so deep in my thoughts, I almost didn't hear the school bus arrive and the voices of other children. I smiled at the sight of them. The house seemed to come alive when they entered, as if it was a big, loving mother opening its arms.

Soon, some curious children came looking for me. I imagined Louise had told them. A small girl with beautiful gold hair and a face that belonged on a doll walked behind an older, taller girl with thick glasses who carried a textbook and notebook. They paused a few feet from me.

"Louise said you just arrived," the girl with the glasses began. "I'm Crystal. This is Janet Taylor. You can think of us as your welcoming committee," she added dryly.

I laughed.

They drew closer.

"My name's Brooke," I said.

"This is actually my favorite spot," Crystal said. "As long as the weather's good, I like to start my homework here."

I nodded and gazed at Janet, who seemed so shy she had to sneak looks at me. I smiled at her, and slowly she smiled back. Then they sat, and the three of us looked out at the lake. The sun was breaking out now, and its rays felt wonderful on my face. It was washing away all the false faces I had worn.

Crystal and Janet stared at me but remained quiet. I knew they had been through the system. We were like soldiers who had fought similar wars and knew that we didn't have to rush to get to know each other. We would have lots of time, because all the promises of new homes that had been made to us would fade in the days to come.

I didn't care. I couldn't think about that now. I was looking beyond the lake.

I could hear all the voices, the cheers, and the screams. I was up at the plate, looking at the pitcher and then back at Coach

Grossbard. She closed her eyes as if in prayer and then opened them and smiled. I took a deep breath and dug in.

Almost as soon as I had hit that ball, I knew it was going to be a home run. It carried my hope with it as it soared higher and higher. I didn't care if I forgot everything else, lost all my recent memories, as long as I could close my eyes and relive that moment.

As long as I could come around those bases toward home.

We hope you have enjoyed this Large Print book. Other G.K. Hall & Co. or Chivers Press Large Print books are available at your library or directly from the publishers.

For more information about current and upcoming titles, please call or write, without obligation, to:

G.K. Hall & Co.
P.O. Box 159
Thorndike, Maine 04986 USA
Tel. (800) 257-5157

OR

Chivers Press Limited
Windsor Bridge Road
Bath BA2 3AX
England
Tel. (0225) 335336

All our Large Print titles are designed for easy reading, and all our books are made to last.